Sweet Cowboy Christmas

A Sweet, Texas Novella

CANDIS TERRY

AVONIMPULSE
An Imprint of HarperCollinsPublishers

Excerpt from *Sweet Surprise* copyright © 2015 by Candis Terry.

Excerpt from *Various States of Undress: Virginia* copyright © 2014 by Laura Simcox.

Excerpt from *The Governess Club: Louisa* copyright © 2014 by Heather Johnson.

Excerpt from *Good Guys Wear Black* copyright © 2014 by Lizbeth Selvig.

Excerpt from *Sinful Rewards 1* copyright © 2014 by Cynthia Sax.

Excerpt from *Covering Kendall* copyright © 2014 by Julie Revell Benjamin.

EPub Edition NOVEMBER 2014 ISBN: 9780062380296
Print Edition ISBN: 9780062380289

10 9 8 7 6 5 4 3

For my readers,
because to me you are all like Christmas morning.

Chapter One

THIRTY-FIVE THOUSAND FEET somewhere above the fly-over states of America, Chase Morgan leaned his head back against the first-class seat and waited for the little bottle of airline whiskey to warm his blood and numb his brain.

"Are you flying alone?" The breathy Marilyn Monroeesque whisper came from the flashy blonde parked in the seat next to him. The same flashy blonde who'd been trying way too hard to get his attention. Though his eyes were closed, it didn't appear she was going to take the hint that he wasn't the least bit interested in adding her name to his private Mile High Club membership.

He mumbled an incoherent response, turned his head toward the window, and tried not to think about the events of the past two weeks that had sent his well-planned life into a death spiral. He also tried not to laugh at the irony that had him zooming away from the snow-covered streets and the high life in New York right back to the land of sweat-stained shirts and dirty boots. Most of all, he tried to ignore the screeching voice of his CEO, which replayed over and over in his head like an annoying Disney movie theme song. Except in his case the catchphrase wasn't "Let it go." Instead it was "You can't quit. You signed a contract." Which promptly crescendoed with the ever-popular, "I'll sue your ass."

Two weeks ago, as a fit and healthy thirty-four-year-old, he'd been at the top of the Madison Avenue game. As a senior ad exec at Brite Minds Worldwide, he'd had an executive office overlooking the Empire State Building, clients others had fought to win over and lost, a Victoria's Secret supermodel girlfriend, and a megamillions Super Bowl ad contract representing the world's top-selling soft drink company waiting to be signed on the dotted line.

He'd had it all.

Until somewhere between his team's campaign presentation that gave a nostalgic nod to mom's apple pie, and handing his Montblanc platinum-line ballpoint to the corporate rep to seal the deal, his heart had decided to skip a beat. Then two. The next thing he knew, he'd woken up in the CCU at Mount Sinai. The twenty-four-hour stay where he'd been poked and prodded, scanned and X-rayed, revealed zip. *Nada.* There had been no blockage. No abnormalities. No disease. And, surprisingly, no damage from the health scare. At least none anyone could see on the exterior.

Nope.

All the damage had been done to the carefully

planned life he'd dreamed about since he'd been a young boy pushing longhorn cattle on his family's ranch in Stephenville, Texas.

Within forty-eight hours of his "episode," his Victoria's Secret supermodel girlfriend dumped him because he now "scared" her. Her exact words poked at him like a playground bully. "What if we're having sex and -you . . . (gasp) . . . died?" His explanations that—most likely—the cardiac event had no lasting effects went unheard. The idea that he could possibly take his last breath while giving her the best sex of her life was just too much for her to handle.

Imagine how he felt.

He wasn't sure she'd be the one he'd want to spend that last breath on anyway. By ten o'clock the following evening, she'd set her so-called broken heart aside and attended a red-carpet event on the arm of Hollywood's newest romantic-comedy heartthrob.

Que sera, sera, sweetheart.

The multimillion-dollar Super Bowl deal he'd worked his ass off for over six months to acquire had been promptly handed over to a rival exec who'd been salivating in the wings, eagerly awaiting an opportunity to pounce like a jackrabbit in heat.

After several more series of tests, his new cardiologist had been unable to explain exactly why he'd had the arrest. Still, the doctor had been clear that while the test results might be inconclusive, stress had many vicious methods of release. One of them was a heart attack.

Stress?

Him?

Ha.

Most nights, after all the late hours behind his desk, he'd had to unwind with a glass of something strong in his hand and a woman on her knees in front of him. Most of his buddies would say that wasn't so terrible.

Too bad it had almost killed him.

Chase closed his ears to the constant chatter of the flashy blonde in the seat next to him as he recalled the doctor's grim advice.

Slow down. Way down. Or I can't guarantee this won't happen again. And next time, you might not be so lucky."

In the ad-agency game of Whack-a-Mole, slowing down didn't exist. If you stopped pedaling, the coyotes would eat you on their way out the door. Chase had given the whole issue a lot of thought. Hell, on doctor's orders, he'd planted his ass on his sofa with nothing to do for a solid week but watch TV shows like *Hoarders* and *Keeping Up with the Kardashians*. By the time he'd finished cringing about what people considered most relevant in life, he'd decided to rethink his future.

Exactly nine days after he'd collapsed across the black granite surface of his executive desk, Chase walked back into the offices of Brite Minds Worldwide, prepared to take the stakes to a different level.

Veronica Cartland, CEO and resident ice queen of Brite Minds Worldwide, had shrieked, "You can't quit! You signed a damn contract. We're in the middle of the busiest season of the year. Christmas is looming, then the Super Bowl. We've got million-dollar deals lined up for weeks. I've been generous enough to let you off the hook for a couple of days. Quit, and I will sue your sorry ass."

Knowing you were necessary enough to be threatened with a lawsuit just because you planned to leave a company felt good, even if your girlfriend found you completely replaceable within a twenty-four-hour time period. Chase had merely smiled at Veronica's outburst, stuck his hands in the pockets of his Armani trousers, and rocked back on his heels. Veronica was young, and beautiful, and the most single-minded, self-centered bitch he'd ever met. She was brilliant at what she did. But if you let her down, she'd serve you up as *au jus* on her steak tartare.

Not once had she asked if he felt better or if the attack had left any long-term effects on his body or psyche.

To her, he wasn't human. He was the machine behind the ebony desk that brought in the revenue so she could afford her Fifth Avenue penthouse view over Manhattan, her custom-designed wardrobe, and the baubles inside the door of the revolving jewelry box also known as Tiffany's.

To him, he didn't want to provide the U.S. government database with yet another statistic, as his own father had done when he died of heart failure at the age of forty-two. Chase wanted to be around for a long time. And though it pained him to give up the dream, the luxury, and everything he'd worked his ass off for, he'd walked out of the building on Madison Avenue with his head held high but still as unemployed as the guy panhandling on the corner of 24th and Park Avenue.

That same night, after fielding concerns from his siblings, his cousin, Abby Morgan, had called from her home-town of Sweet, Texas, when she'd learned of his health scare. In her soft Southern twang, she'd coerced him into coming for a visit. Shucking his wool coat for a little warm sunshine and fresh air at this wintry time of year sounded like a good idea. Of course, he'd intended it to be on the sands of a tropical beach. Still, he'd always adored his cousins Abby and Annie and thought maybe dropping in for a couple of days to say hello wouldn't be a bad idea.

The truth of the matter was that a quick stop in Sweet took him one step closer to home. The home he hadn't been back to in well over a decade. The home where the brother and sister he loved still resided. The home where his father had died and taken Chase's heart with him to the grave.

Sweet, Texas, was less than a four-hour drive away from the home he'd once loved so much.

The question was: Would he find the courage to return?

Next thing he knew, he'd been standing in the TSA line at LaGuardia on the first day of December, with a boarding pass in hand. No hurry to go anywhere. No hurry to get back to New York. For the first time in almost ten years, he'd be spending the Christmas holi-day somewhere other than Manhattan. He'd avoid the freezing snow, the gargantuan tree lighting in Rockefeller Center, the extravagant window displays, and the harried shoppers.

Thank God.

Back in Stephenville, when he'd been a boy tearing

open his presents on Christmas morning alongside his brother and sister, he never imagined he'd develop such an aversion for the holiday or that his chosen career would make him view the celebration from behind such a cynical pair of eyes.

But that's what had happened.

When the flashy blonde in the seat next to him ran her manicured finger down his arm, and sang, "Wakey, wakey, hot stuff," he pretended to be asleep. He didn't normally turn down an attractive offer with absolutely no strings attached.

Times had changed. And he had a lot of thinking to do.

Because for the first time in his life, he didn't have a dream, and he didn't have a plan.

LAST-MINUTE BOOKINGS AT the Magic Box Guest Ranch in Sweet, Texas, were rare. Last-minute bookings for the first week of December were unheard of. Most visitors preferred to time their vacations for midspring, so they could try to catch the beauty of the bluebonnets that blanketed the meadows, or even the newborn calves and foals that frolicked in the fields while their mothers grazed nearby. Most chose springtime to avoid the blistering heat of a Texas summer.

Faith Walker glanced up at the western-star clock above the bookcase in her office and wondered exactly when her one-and-only guest for the next ten days would see fit to arrive.

Had it not been for her sister Paige calling in a favor for their good friend Abby Morgan, who was busy working on her wedding plans to marry Jackson—one of the notorious and good-looking Wilder brothers—Faith would have rejected the reservation. With only three weeks until Christmas, she already had plenty on her plate to do for her annual fund-raiser to support the summer camp she provided for underprivileged children.

The first year she'd taken over for her uncle Charles had been when he'd become ill. He'd given her the freedom to do as she saw fit, so she'd opened the gates of the Magic Box Ranch to the children for a week. At the time, it had been merely a cattle ranch with an enormous main lodge house and a few ranch-hand cabins. The private lake and running creek added extra charm and opportunity for some kid-style fun. When her uncle passed and left her the place, she'd changed things up quick—giving to those who couldn't always give to themselves. Namely the children. Especially those who wanted to reach for the stars but didn't know how or have the means. Those in particular held a special place in her heart.

The Country Christmas fund-raiser she held the week before the big holiday had become something of a tradition around Sweet the past few years. With the generosity of the close-knit community, it had become quite successful too. Which was only one of the reasons she was in a big hurry to get on with her plans to make it even bigger, better, brighter, and more successful than last year. Time was a wasting. She didn't have the luxury to babysit yet another high-powered, snooty executive who wanted to play cowboy for a week while being pampered with the ranch's famous gourmet feasts and personal massage therapist.

Having already given her staff the time off for the holidays, she'd had to make phone calls last night to put everyone on standby. With the exception of old Bull Crothers, who kept an eye on the livestock year-round and lived in one of the ancient bunkhouses her uncle Charles had built for the ranch hands years ago, the place was pretty much deserted.

Her sister Paige, who still considered herself a newly-wed after a year of marriage to Aiden Marshall, worried about her being alone so much. Faith didn't mind it at all. The quiet months gave her time to recuperate after a busy season bustling with the spoiled-executive elite she catered to. Their sometimes outrageous demands never ceased to amaze.

Caviar at midnight? Sure.

A hot-stone massage to soothe away the stress because a rabbit ran out in front of you on the trail? No problem.

The Magic Box Guest Ranch provided whatever the guest needed. With a few exceptions. Texas might be a part of the Wild Wild West, but they did not provide ladies of the night for a gentleman's entertainment. And they didn't do wee-morning-hour runs to the drive-thru liquor store to hunt up a bottle of some kind of cognac no one in Texas had ever even heard of. But that was mostly because the drive-thru liquor store was closed.

With the lodge house currently quiet except for the incessant panting of Doc Holiday, her faithful, patient, and uniquely relaxed for the usually hyper breed, Border Collie, the sound of tires on the gravel road that led to the house was easy to pick up.

"Oh joy, Doc. Looks like we've got company," Faith said to the dog, who cocked his head as if to say, "Company? Now?" Which would be followed by Doc's never-ending ear-tipping request for "Bacon?"

"Come on, buddy. Off-season or not, we need to give this guest an extraspecial welcome, being that he's related to our good friends Abby and Annie." Doc gave a dog grunt as he got up off his pooch pillow and followed her into the registration and activities office.

Moments later, the door opened and a cool breeze blew in alongside a man who'd be likely to make most females' mouths water. He was tall, dark, and athletically lean, with sexy-as-sin green eyes set in a face that would fit perfectly on one of those man-candy calendars eighty-plus-year-old Arlene Potter kept on the living room wall in her little rock bungalow on Bluebonnet Lane.

For a brief flash of insanity, Faith wished she'd bothered to put on a little blush and mascara that morning or brushed her hair instead of sticking it up in a ponytail and hiding the rest beneath a ball cap.

With a hard blink, she resumed business mode to deliver the same courtesy everyone else received when they walked through that door—a Texas-sized helping of good old Southern hospitality.

Except, what could you really say to someone who'd shown up at a dude ranch looking like he'd just stepped out of a Times Square billboard?

"WELCOME TO THE Magic Box Ranch."

Chase dropped his suitcase by the door, where he was greeted by a woman a bit on the shorter side and definitely a little on the healthier side of the women he usually met up with in NYC. Not that she was fat. And he wouldn't exactly call her plump. But from where he stood just inside the door, he could tell she filled out the black T-shirt and pair of Wranglers with luscious curves unlike the waifish, famished-looking creatures he'd seen strut the catwalk at Fashion Week.

Her sun-streaked brown hair was pulled up in a ponytail that stuck out through the hole at the back of a pink-and-black "Cowgirl" ball cap and shadowed a sweetheart face. A worn and scuffed pair of brown boots finished off a look that touted her as a workingwoman and not just someone who sat behind a desk filing papers.

He'd become so accustomed to city women who dressed for the masses that he'd forgotten about the women he'd grown up knowing. Those who mostly wore jeans and boots, denim and cotton. Those who dressed not with the hopes that their photo might end up on *ET's Hottest Fashions of the Week*, but of necessity and common sense.

When she came around the desk to shake his hand, he got a better view. And it was a nice one.

"My name's Faith Walker," she said through plump, kissable lips that revealed the slightest hint of dimples when she smiled. Her dark gray eyes were direct, no-nonsense, and would most likely cut through the layers of BS someone tried to spoon-feed her.

Faith was what he and his friends back in the day would call a *hot damn real woman*.

He came forward, shook her extended hand, and smiled when he discovered she had a firm grip. None of that three-fingered loosey-goosey thing he'd run into with women before.

"Chase Morgan." Surprised by the impulse to reel her in closer, he reluctantly let go of her hand.

"I'm going to apologize right from the start, Mr. Morgan." She flashed him those dimples, then went around to the business side of the desk and began tapping on a computer keyboard. "We really don't get guests this time of year. So the place is empty, and I'm afraid you won't have others to share conversation or company."

She punched the RETURN key and looked up. "However, you will still receive the same amenities we offer the rest of the year, with the exception of the pool, which we closed for the season last month. The hot tub is available, though, as are the trail rides, fishing pond, and a whole lot of front-porch sittin'. We offer fine dining you can either enjoy in the privacy of your cabin, or you're welcome to eat here at the main lodge. If y'all have any specific dietary needs or you have a certain meal request, please feel free to let me know, and I'll be sure our chef accommodates you."

"I'll eat anything. No dietary restrictions." Thank God. He already maintained a fairly healthy lifestyle, but with recent events, he'd decided to step everything up a notch. *After* his ten days of R&R. "Whatever is served will work just fine."

For the first time since he'd arrived, he managed to tear his eyes off Faith and look around the office. The décor delivered the predictable Texas-ranch flavor without all the hokeyness of the fictional jackalope or an armadillo-shell flowerpot.

The Texas stars and rope accents had been accentuated with the telltale signs of the impending Christmas holiday. A garland of artificial evergreen dotted with pinecones and dried berries had been draped around the reception desk, and a small statue of Old Saint Nick in Western wear sat on top of the counter. The scent of gingerbread wafted throughout the room from some kind of warming device near the miniature tree, which had been decorated with small tin stars and miniature red horseshoes.

Something sneezed, and Chase looked down to find a black-and-white cattle dog sitting at his feet. "Hey, boy." He hunkered down to pet the dog on the head. "What's your name?"

"That's Doc. He's not your typical cow dog. In fact, he's pretty lazy. But he makes a great hiking companion if you need one."

"Thanks. I might take him up on that." Chase smiled, righted himself, and looked into those pretty gray eyes. "I haven't had a dog for a long time."

Her head went back. Just slightly. But enough to let him know she was completely surprised that he . . . what? That he'd even had a dog?

"Something wrong?" he asked.

"You just don't seem the type."

"What *type* is that?"

"A dog person." She shoved some papers into a brochure and thrust it at him. "I mean, I know people in New York City own dogs, I just feel bad for the animals that get stuck inside a small apartment all day."

"Nice sentiment," he said. "But you really don't know anything about me or where I came from, do you?" The slow Southern drawl he'd traded long ago for the brisk lingo of the East Coast wouldn't give him away either.

When she shook her head, that long ponytail swung gently across her back. "Abby didn't say much to my sister other than you were looking for a place to land for a few days to let the . . ."

Her hesitation piqued his interest. "Go ahead and say what you're thinking." As a man who loved honesty and one who was enjoying the hell out of this lively conversation, he smiled. Things here were getting more interesting by the minute.

"She said that y'all needed a place to let the stink of the city off you for a few days. Sorry." She waved a dismissive hand. "I still haven't learned to disengage my brain from my mouth. I get in trouble for it all the time."

He laughed. "No need to apologize. And you're right. That's exactly what I'm looking for."

"Well. Then you've come to the right place." From a pegged board behind the desk, she removed a skeleton key that looked too old to open anything. Then she came around the desk and headed toward the door. "I put you up in our nicest cabin being as you're related to a good friend."

"I appreciate that."

"No extra charge."

"Appreciate that too." Although he'd walked away from his job, he had more than enough to keep him going for several years if he chose. He could afford months of *front-porch sittin'* at the Magic Box Guest Ranch. But he wasn't about to share that bit of information with someone he'd just met.

When she grasped the handle of his suitcase, he reached out to stop her. "I can carry my own bag."

She looked up with surprise.

Was she kidding? He might have almost died a few weeks ago, but the hell if he'd let himself be treated like some pansy-ass who couldn't carry his own damn luggage.

"You sure?" Her head cocked just slightly, and her dark eyes took a quick trip over his body. "Most folks of your . . . status who come here expect to be given the VIP treatment."

The diss was so slight he barely recognized it. At the same time, the snub gave him a clear indication that while the Magic Box Guest Ranch might cater to the highly paid influential type, Faith herself might very well–ironically–be a bit of a snob in that direction. If so, why didn't she just get a job somewhere else, so she didn't have to put up with them?

"Again, you don't really know me or my background so . . ." He left the rest unspoken, knowing she was a smart cookie and would get his meaning.

She signaled him to follow her out the door and onto the large, covered veranda that surrounded at least three sides of the huge lodge house built from sturdy pine logs. Boughs of evergreen were starting to make an appearance within the clever assortment of Texas paraphernalia set up in niches here and there. A classic country look made all the more inviting by a long procession of rocking chairs painted in Texas flag hues of red, white, and blue.

Regardless of Faith's obvious distaste for the Brooks Brothers set, Chase didn't mind letting her walk ahead of him. The choice had nothing to do with the fact that he didn't know where to go and everything to do with the way her hips swayed in those skintight Wranglers.

"You're right." Her delayed response came as she led the way across the dry patch of earth where little puffs of dust kicked up in the wake of her boots. "I don't know you or your background."

Chase fought a grin at her inability to zip her lip. And he wondered how she managed to keep a job that obviously left a bitter taste in that pretty mouth.

He also noticed she didn't apologize for her blunder.

She guided him down a gravel path beneath a canopy of the far-reaching branches of live oak. Along the path, heat-tolerant shrubs and clumps of prickly pear cacti vied for dominance.

A spiny lizard darted across their path. When most girls would have screamed, Faith merely stopped to let the small reptile pass. Impressed, Chase fondly remembered the contests he'd have with his brother Boone to see who could catch the most lizards. Once their little sister Cassidy would supervise the tail count, they'd let them all go to be caught again another day.

The memory reminded him that from the moment he'd stepped foot in the Lone Star State, revisiting his family roots during his stay would need to be addressed.

Or not.

Farther down the gravel path, Faith stepped up onto the wide porch of a small cabin that resembled an old Western saloon. The only thing missing was a pair of swinging doors and a working girl hanging on a post out front. So authentic was the aged wood building, he could almost hear someone inside tickling the ivories with a lively ragtime rendition of "Buffalo Gals."

Faith moved aside a fencepost snowman with the toe of her boot as she stuck the skeleton key in the lock and gave it a twist. When the door swung open, she motioned for him to step inside, where the scent of warm sugar cookies greeted him. He was surprised, and delighted, to find a sizable interior with a compact kitchen, dining area, king-sized bed, and sitting area all rolled into one. In a separate room was a fully upgraded bath with a whirlpool tub and a Rainforest shower system.

The cabin décor was unquestionably Western, with red gingham curtains framing the windows with rusty horseshoe tiebacks. It had also been decked out for the holiday, with a small Christmas tree in the corner of the room that glowed with tiny white lights, plus various other holiday decorations placed in strategic locations. Even a gingham-accented garland hung across the gas fireplace mantel.

From the center of the room, Faith made a wide sweep with her hand, spouting the amenities such as air-conditioning, a microwave, and a refrigerator supplied with everything from milk, eggs, and butter, to several ramekins filled with fresh quiche. Sodas and bottled water were also provided, as well as a fully stocked bar. On the rustic kitchen table was a bowl of fresh fruit and a platter of cookies.

Hell, with everything available right here, he wouldn't have to leave the cabin for days.

Once Faith finished her well-rehearsed spiel, she turned to him with a smile that accented those delicious dimples and handed him the key.

"It's past suppertime," she said, tucking both hands behind her back, which in his favor, thrust her ample bosom in his direction. "But if you're hungry, I can rustle up something in the kitchen for you to eat."

"I'd hate to bother you," he said, fearing his empty stomach would growl any second. "But I haven't had anything to eat since last night."

"It's no bother. Our chef, Shelby, cooked a tender pot roast today, and there's also a fresh loaf of Ciabatta. I'd be happy to put together a couple of sandwiches and a salad and bring it out to you."

"Have you eaten?"

She blinked. "Pardon me?"

"Have you eaten dinner?"

"No ... uh ... I was too busy getting everything ready for your arrival."

"You mentioned I could either have my meals here

or at the lodge house. How about I meet you there after I take a shower and freshen up a little? You know." He flashed a smile. "To get the stink of the city off me."

"Ssssure." Briefly, she turned away as though something he'd said had thrown her off-balance. When she came back around, she'd rediscovered her cool and her professionalism. "Your meal will be ready whenever you are. Just come through the big double doors. The dining hall will be on your right."

"Does the staff eat in the dining hall?"

"No. We prefer the kitchen."

"Then I'll meet you in the kitchen."

"Oh." Her gaze dropped from his eyes to his mouth, then slowly crawled back up with a definite pull of confusion to the center of her delicate brows.

She turned to go, then abruptly stopped at the door. "I meant to apologize earlier for my careless judgment of you. I'll admit it was quite presumptuous. But honestly, Mr. Morgan, if you choose not to be judged as one of *those* types of clients, you really shouldn't show up to a cattle ranch wearing an expensive sport jacket and loafers."

Chapter Two

SOMETIMES IT TOOK a long, hot shower to make a man feel whole again. Sometimes it took a shot of whiskey. Sometimes it took a few well-spent hours with a hot-blooded female. For a change, Chase enjoyed the long, hot shower—alone—and waived the shot of whiskey in favor of a bottle of water. Not quite the way he would have managed his time a few short weeks ago.

Although he'd made a deliberate decision to quit his job and slow the hectic pace of his life, he had no intention of becoming the guy who drank wheat-grass smoothies by choice, gave up heart-pounding sex, or refused the occasional celebratory bottle of champagne. The current situation had nothing to do with his health and everything to do with wanting to be at the top of his game when he, once again, came face-to-face with the openly opinionated Faith Walker.

During their brief conversation, she'd bested him too

many times before she'd blown out of his cabin like a sexy Texas tornado and left him scratching his head. He wasn't familiar with that concept, and he was pretty sure he didn't favor it.

He had mastered boardroom domination. He was the fast-talking, smooth negotiator who had made billions of dollars for Brite Minds Worldwide even before he'd turned the age of thirty. He'd sweet-talked supermodels into his bed and drank beer with friends on celebrity row at the Knicks games.

So how the hell had he let one little slip of a Southern girl best him at his own game?

With any luck, dinner would prove to be highly entertaining.

He smiled as he closed the cabin door behind him without locking it. He highly doubted there was anyone for miles who'd be tempted to use their five-finger-discount skills to snatch the grinning snowman perched on his mantel. Other than his Rolex, he hadn't brought anything of value with him. Quite the contrary. At the last minute, he'd tossed a few items from his old wardrobe in his suitcase, then wondered why he'd held on to them all these years.

Nostalgia? He wasn't that kind of guy.

In fact, he'd been called quite the opposite on many occasions. This might run counter to some of the curious observations friends had made over the years, but the one that made him question his own heart and the reason why he hadn't been home in well over a decade remained locked away.

Night had fallen, and the short hike beneath the canopy of live oaks revealed a pathway lit by small lanterns and tiny white lights that flickered like lightning bugs in the bordering trees and bushes. Chase didn't think these were just Christmas decorations, but they definitely added to the mood of the impending holiday. Maybe before he'd been too wrapped up in the sexy sway of Faith's Wranglers, but as he strolled down the path toward the big lodge house, he noticed things he hadn't caught the first time. Or maybe Faith had just been a busy girl while he'd taken that long, hot, solitary shower.

A tractor-tire-sized evergreen wreath with red berry holly hung just below the towering peak of the barn roof. Boughs and garlands bearing pinecones and white lights decorated the archway of the veranda surrounding the lodge house. And two identical wreaths brightened the large double doors. The holiday décor didn't have a finished feel to it. More like someone had just gotten started.

A sigh pushed from his lungs. He didn't know why he thought he'd be able to escape the whole ho-ho-ho merriment when he'd left New York. Probably he was the only one who never caught the *spirit* that everyone else seemed to get at this time of year. Hell, for as long as he'd lived in New York, he'd never gotten the spirit. And that was damned hard to do when the city did a hell of a job to make itself shiny and bright. But for him, the season full of cheery salutations, bright, shiny packages, eggnog, and sappy Hallmark movies only brought the painful reminder of his father's death on that fateful Christmas morning.

He'd been eighteen at the time and home from his first year at college. His brother Boone had been in his junior year of high school. And little sister Cassidy had been a freshman. All three of them had gathered in the kitchen early to make coffee and breakfast for their parents before the traditional ripping-open-of-the-packages began. From the master bedroom their mother's blood-curdling scream caused Cassidy to drop the glass coffee carafe, Boone to slice his finger while chopping onions, and Chase to burn himself on the cast-iron skillet.

Like the Keystone Cops, they'd tangled up in the hall-way in their rush to find the source of the problem.

But they were too late.

Sometime during the night, while Santa had been ho-ho-hoing down chimneys to deliver gifts, their father had taken his last breath. A massive coronary had claimed him at the young age of forty-two on a day that should have been a celebration.

That had been the last Christmas Chase had acknowl-edged the holiday. It had also been one of the very last times he'd stepped foot in the home where their beloved father had left them all behind without a last good-bye.

As Chase stepped up on the veranda and a HOME FOR CHRISTMAS doormat welcomed him, the sense of loss became overwhelming. His chest tightened, and he grabbed at the front of his shirt while he inhaled a deep breath to clear the miserable clog.

Irony was a caustic witch.

He'd loved the big, rambling, ranch-style home he'd grown up in. A home that had been decorated and filled with more love than money. The memories of those happier times were so rich and so real, he could almost reach out and touch his daddy's face. Those recollections clung to every corner of the house, barn, and corral. Unable to face the constant reminders, he'd never gone back.

On occasion, Boone and Cassidy had come to visit him in the Big Apple, as did his mother. But it wasn't the same. It was like their father was the glue that linked them all together.

And then his mother remarried.

It wasn't that Chase hadn't liked Butch Reynolds, the man his mother had married, the man just made it difficult. At first it seemed as though Butch tried too hard to step into their daddy's shoes. Then just as fast, Butch changed his mind and couldn't be bothered with his new wife's *adult* children. Next thing they knew, their mother had put the ranch up for sale and was moving to Dallas.

Neither Chase nor either of his siblings had wanted to see their daddy's hard work thrown away. So between the three of them, they'd come up with the money for the down payment, and their uncle cosigned on the loan. Though Chase had paid off that loan with his first incentive bonus, he remained a silent partner in the business and accepted none of the profits. At their insistence, Boone and Cassidy continued to put his share in a savings account. Though he never thought he'd need the money, it might very well come in handy now.

Sweet was only a few hours away from Stephenville.

Maybe he should forge ahead with his new lease on life with a little hometown visit.

A nice thought, but the knot wound tight in the pit of his stomach knew the truth.

He might never go back.

Wiping the soles of his shoes on the HOME FOR CHRISTMAS doormat, he knocked on the big door of the lodge house, then remembered what Faith had said about just coming in. Turning the knob, he stepped inside a huge foyer, where a piped-in George Strait singing "Winter Wonderland" and the scent of warm gingerbread cookies seemed to flow from every direction. Chase refrained from rolling his eyes at the overload of cheer.

Tail wagging, Doc met him at the door. When the Border Collie looked up with his big brown eyes, Chase knelt to give him a little attention. Apparently the dog wasn't too shy to drop to the ground and roll to his back for a belly rub. Chase finished with a quick pat between Doc's pointy ears, then went in search of his dinner partner.

A hotly exclaimed and very un-Christmasy F-bomb exploded above George Strait's sleigh bells ringing. As Chase came around the dividing wall he found Faith on the very top rung of an aluminum ladder, tongue caught between her teeth, and stretching to place a punched-tin star at the top of a Christmas tree that must have been all of ten feet tall.

Chase's heart gave a hard thump against his ribs as Faith began to lose her balance, and the ladder wobbled beneath her scuffed brown boots. No thought, all action, he made it to the bottom of the ladder in less than the blink of an eye. He reached to steady the ladder but was too late. Butt first, she tumbled into his arms with a surprised "Oof."

Utter shock brightened her gray eyes. For a moment, as he held her safe and secure in his arms, they just looked at each other. Reality finally sank in, and embarrassment highlighted her cheeks.

"You play football?" she snapped in lieu of a *thank you for saving my bacon*.

"Running back. High school and college."

"Thought for sure you'd have been a wide receiver." A soft sigh lifted her luscious breasts as she gave his chest a quick little pat. "Nice catch."

Before he set her on her feet, he noticed how good she felt in his arms. Warm. Soft. Curvy. Nice. She smelled good too. Like sweet gingerbread and creamy hot chocolate. Which only led to him wondering how she'd taste.

Jesus.

He didn't even know the woman. He certainly had no business thinking things like that or even the followup thoughts that made him wonder exactly what a man could do with a warm, soft, curvy, delicious-smelling, tasty woman and a bottle of chocolate.

"Damn good thing too," he said. "Or someone would be calling 9-1-1. What the hell were you thinking?"

Then, and only then, did he notice she still held the tin star in her hand.

"I was thinking I needed to get this star on the top of the tree."

"Or what, your boss would get mad? Doesn't he have someone else who's taller and—"

Her hands went to her shapely hips, and he feared she'd stab her nice soft skin with that ridiculous ornament. "Why would you immediately assume my boss is a man?"

Yeah. Why would he? Especially when the boss for whom he'd just busted his can had been a woman.

"Guess it's my turn to be presumptuous." He folded his arms. "Which doesn't answer my question of what you were doing standing on tiptoe on the top step of a ladder. Didn't you read the sticker that says not to go any higher than the second step from the top?"

"The tree is taller than I remember. Last year, Danny Joe was still here, and—"

"Who's Danny Joe?" And why did he feel the slightest bit jealous?

"Probably the most important staff member we have. Or I should say had. He just signed with the Mavs." She sighed. "All six feet six inches of him. Our loss is professional basketball's gain. Guess I'm going to have to get a taller ladder."

"Or maybe you could just get a shorter tree."

"Now why would we want to do that? Haven't you heard?" Her dimples flashed. "Everything's bigger in Texas."

Her expression was so smug, he hated to spoil her fun and break the news that he had ten generations of Texas blood running thick through his veins. Let her presume he was a city boy with no knowledge of the Lone Star

State, ranching, or even dogs for that matter. Maybe for the past ten years, he'd played that part. But a few weeks ago all that had changed in a heartbeat.

Literally.

"I have heard that. Always wondered exactly what it referred to other than the distance that seems to take forever to get anywhere."

"Oh. You know." She looked down at the tin star still in her hand, then she brought those smoky eyes back up to his face. "Big state. Big ranches. Big steaks. Big hair. Big Bullshitters."

He laughed.

"By the way, thank you for catching me. I'd hated to have seen the bruise that fall would have left."

"More than likely you could have added some broken bones to your list as well."

"Whew." Those delicious dimples of hers flashed again. "Lucky you were here then."

He was starting to think the same thing.

"How about I put that up on top of the tree for you?" He offered not because he cared about any part of the ridiculous holiday rituals people stuck to but because he knew if he didn't, she'd climb right back up on that ladder again.

"That would be real hospitable of you."

In all the years he'd stomped his boots across the dry, often cracked, soil of his daddy's farm, he'd never once thought about the accent that belonged uniquely to the Lone Star State. But when Faith let out that slow, sexy, Texas drawl, he noticed.

When she handed him the star, their fingers touched. Unless he was losing his mind, which, as certain events of the past weeks would suggest was entirely possible, he would swear there had been a snap of electricity between them.

Without further delving into the possibilities of physical attraction or the loss of mental capacity, he climbed the ladder and easily set the star on top of the tree. On the way down, he noticed that, with the exception of little white lights, the rest of the tree was bare of ornamentation. When his feet hit the hardwood floor, he noticed the mountain of boxes piled up all around the room. Hell, he finally noticed the room.

Guess there was nothing like a beautiful woman falling into one's arms to diminish the impact of a grand room accented by pine and stone with a spectacular view of the tree-covered hills through an enormous picture window. The stone fireplace hearth was massive. Above his head was an impressive antler chandelier. And the furnishings were casual leather with nail-head trim. All in all, it was the type of room, regardless how massive, that invited someone to come in, kick their feet up, and sit a spell.

"What's with all the boxes?" he asked, dreading the answer.

"Christmas decorations."

Figured.

"Takes about a week to get everything put in place. Then it seems like it's time to take them all down again. Sometimes I wonder why we don't just leave them up."

"So why put them up at all?"

Her head whipped around. "Don't tell me you're one of those anti-Christmas people." Her nose wrinkled as if she smelled something rotten. "Of course you are. You, who are able to experience the wonder of the holiday with all those beautiful city lights, and magic, and snow . . . do you realize I've never had a white Christmas? Of course you don't know. How could you? You're too anti-Christmas."

"How could I know you've never had a white Christmas when I really don't know you?"

"Well, there is that." She bent down and opened the flaps of a cardboard box. "Exactly what is it that you do in the big city anyway?"

Somehow, she managed to keep derision out of the inquiry. Which, he was sure, must have been quite the chore. And since she genuinely seemed at least fairly interested, he kept it simple by saying, "I worked for a Madison Avenue advertising agency."

"Worked? As in past tense?"

Okay, he hadn't actually meant to give her that much information. "I'm taking a sabbatical."

"Don't most of your people take their sabbaticals to the Hamptons or something?"

"In the summer. Although I'm not really one of *those* people."

"Hmmm."

When most people gave something considerable thought, their faces showed little or no emotion. He'd been the king of never showing his hand. Faith's expressions were not only readable; they were a breath of fresh air. If she even tried to lie, she'd be caught in a second.

"*My* people usually go to Florida or the Caribbean," he said.

"And yet you chose Texas?"

"Maybe it's easier to say Texas chose me."

"How so?"

He studied the curiosity on her face.

Nope.

Not going to go there.

"I can help you unpack all these boxes if you want," he said, expertly diverting her interest. "I'd never forgive myself if you climbed up on that ladder again and fell."

"I usually don't climb ladders to unpack boxes." A smile tickled her lips. "So I guess what you're saying is you'd be thrilled to help me unpack the boxes and decorate the tree?"

Had he said that? Or had she been tippling the eggnog?

"Or maybe you're too tired from that long flight from New York."

Hell no. He might be tired, but it wasn't from a damned flight. He had a life hangover. And while it would be easy to use that as an excuse, the idea of hanging around her and her sassy tongue for a while sounded a whole lot more interesting than hitting the sheets alone.

"I'd be happy to help." He'd also become quite skilled at a brazen lie.

Her head tilted, and that ponytail swayed just slightly. "Dinner first?"

Whatever possessed him to reach out and pull the ball

cap off her head, he didn't know. But that's exactly what he did.

"Hey." She smoothed her hand over the top of her head. "I'm having a bad hair day."

"Looks great to me." He tossed the cap on the coffee table. "I like being able to look into a person's eyes when I'm talking to them."

"That have anything to do with not trusting folks?"

Nope. It had everything to do with his just wanting to see her better.

"I don't have trust issues," he said. "And dinner can wait."

Two hours into tree decorating, Faith looked across the room where Chase stood holding a pinecone Santa in one hand and a marshmallow snowman ornament in the other. The grim expression on his face made her laugh.

He looked up. "What's so funny?"

"You look confused."

"I never knew there were so many different forms a Santa and a snowman could take on."

"Oh, wait until you get to the button angels. They're adorable."

"Buttons?"

She nodded. "My kids made them. We even have pipe-cleaner snowflakes packed in here somewhere."

"Your kids?" His expression went dark. "You're married?"

"Not that kind of *my kids*. They're the kids that the

Magic Box Ranch sponsors for a few weeks during summer and at Christmastime," she explained, and was surprised when his expression brightened, and he appeared oddly relieved.

"I just get a little attached and end up calling them *my* kids. When they're here for summer camp, one of the projects we do is to have a Christmas in July craft. Usually, the challenge is for them to make an ornament to hang on the tree." She lifted several marshmallow snowmen from the box and hung them on the lower branches.

"We've been doing this for several years now, which is why there are so many to unpack. Sometimes they get carried away because it's fun. And sometimes they just get competitive."

"Charity work is important," he said. "How do you find the funds?"

"Why do you think the ranch caters exclusively to the elite?"

His sensuous mouth turned up into a smile. "Very clever."

She shrugged and hung a gold spray-painted cardboard star next to a pipe-cleaner candy cane. "Hardworking families usually can't afford what we charge. So for a few weeks of the year, we open the doors to them and also to underprivileged or disabled children so that they can enjoy a slice of the Western way of life."

Chase had come up to stand beside her and hand her more ornaments. While most of the influential men who visited the ranch usually reeked of overpowering aftershave, Chase wore the scent of warm man and clean cotton. Tonight, when he'd shown up in a pair of black slacks and a black T- shirt, she'd had to find a composure that had nothing to do with his rescuing her.

She'd taken a fall all right.

For him.

Broken her own damn rules is what she'd done. Hadn't she learned her lesson? Men with pockets full of change they threw around like penny candy at a parade weren't the kind she could ever be interested in.

At least never again.

Trouble was, Chase Morgan was an extremely sexy man with bedroom eyes and a smile that said he could deliver on anything he'd promise in that direction. Broad shoulders that confirmed he could carry the weight of the world if need be. And big, capable hands that had already proven they could catch her if she fell.

He was trouble.

And she had no doubt she was *in* trouble.

Best to keep to the subject of the charity work and leave the drooling for some yummy, untouchable movie star like Chris Hemsworth or Mark Wahlberg.

Discreetly, she moved to the other side of the tree and hung a pinecone Santa on a higher branch. "We also hold a winter fund-raiser, which is what I'm preparing for now."

"What kind of fund-raiser?" he asked from right beside her again, with that delicious male scent tickling her nostrils.

"We hold it the week before Christmas. It's a barn dance, bake sale, auction, and craft fair all rolled into one." She escaped to the other side of the tree, but he showed up again, hands full of dangling ornaments. "Last year we raised $25,000. I'd like to top that this year if possible."

"You must have a large committee to handle all that planning."

She laughed.

Dark brows came together over those green eyes that had flashes of gold and copper near their centers. "So I gather you're not just the receptionist-slash–tree decorator."

"I have a few other talents I put to good use around here."

"Now you've really caught my interest."

To get away from the intensity in his gaze, she climbed up the stepstool and placed a beaded-heart ornament on the tree. She could only imagine how he probably used that intensity to cut through the boardroom bullshit.

As a rule, she never liked the clientele to know she was the sole owner of the ranch. Even though society should be living in this more open-minded century, there were those who believed it was still a man's world.

"Oh, it's really nothing that special," she said. "Just some odds and ends here and there."

When she came down the stepstool, his hands went to her waist to provide stability. At least that's what she told herself, even after those big warm palms lingered when she'd turned around to face him.

"Fibber," he said while they were practically nose to nose.

"I beg your pardon?"

"You know what I do for a living, Faith? How I've been so successful? I read people. I come up with an idea, then I read people for how they're going to respond. Going into a pitch, I know whether they're likely to jump on board or whether I need to go straight to plan B."

His grip around her waist tightened, and the fervor with which he studied her face sent a shiver racing down her spine. There was nothing threatening in his eyes or the way his thumbs gently caressed the area just above the waistband of her Wranglers.

Quite the opposite.

"You have the most expressive face I've ever seen," he declared. "And when you're stretching the truth, you can't look someone in the eye. Dead giveaway."

"And you've known me for what? All of five minutes?" she protested.

One corner of his masculine lips slowly curved into a smile. "Guess that's just me being presumptuous again."

Everything female in Faith's body awakened from the death sleep she'd put it in after she'd discovered the man she'd been just weeks away from marrying, hadn't been the man she'd thought him to be at all.

"Looks like we're both a little too trigger-happy in the jumping-the-gun department," she said, while deftly extricating herself from his grasp even as her body begged her to stay put.

"Maybe."

Backing away, she figured she'd tempted herself enough for one night. Best they get dinner over with before she made some grievous error in judgment she'd never allow herself to forget.

She clapped her hands together. "So . . . how about we get to that dinner?"

"Sounds great." His gaze wandered all over her face and body. "I'm getting hungrier by the second."

Whoo boy.

Chapter Three

WAKING TO THE sound of absolute silence wasn't something Chase was used to anymore. Well, he'd take that back. There had been birds chirping and the occasional moo of a disgruntled heifer, so he guessed that counted as something. But it was far different from the usual taxi horns honking or emergency-vehicle sirens he heard from his Manhattan apartment. For over an hour, he'd lain in bed like a big, lazy slug with his hands tucked behind his head, looking up at the pressed-tin ceiling. He had no clients to be thinking about. No difficulties with his boss or coworkers.

He had nothing.

Yet as he lay there craving a hot cup of coffee, he had plenty occupying his thoughts. Namely the woman he'd spent hours with last night accomplishing the mundane task of trimming a Christmas tree while listening to a selection of holiday tunes sung by popular country artists.

He'd tried not to Grinch out on her even though, after a while, it all became a bit too much. He'd handled it fine until "White Christmas" played.

The song had been his father's favorite.

Until that moment, as he stood inside the grand living room alongside Faith, sticking ornaments on the tree, he'd refused to listen to the song. For a moment, he'd felt trapped. Claustrophobic. A terrific weight had settled in his chest until he could barely breathe. The spell had been shattered when Faith had rested her hand on top of his and smiled. It was as if she could sense his panic. But that was ridiculous. How could she possibly know?

That small salvation had been the last skin-to-skin contact they'd had. From that moment, she'd kept her distance. He didn't blame her. During the decorating—whether it was helping her down from the ladder or leaning in to help her position an ornament—he'd stolen every opportunity to touch her. Being a well-raised Southern girl, she most likely thought his actions inappropriate. But he hadn't been able to help himself. The first time she'd ended up in his arms unexpectedly. The rest of the time had all been conscious intent on his part.

He hadn't just wanted to touch her, he'd *had* to touch her. It was the craziest damn thing he'd ever experienced. One second he was being a typical guy and appreciating the view she gave him when she climbed up on that stepstool, the next second his hands were tingling with a desire he hadn't been able to control.

When they'd gone into the kitchen for hot roast beef sandwiches, things hadn't calmed down any. As they sat at the table across from each other, he'd wanted to move his chair closer. Every smile she threw his way he caught like Johnny Bench with the biggest catcher's mitt on earth. He'd gotten to know her a little. Maybe not in the way he'd have liked, but he found her as interesting as she was sexy. He knew that putting on the flirt wasn't her style, yet somehow she managed to do it so effortlessly, he couldn't help be drawn in.

This morning, when Chase enthusiastically headed to the lodge house to grab a cup of coffee, he discovered an elderly man, with what looked like at least a hundred years of character lines on his face, in one of the rockers on the veranda. The thin man's snap-front Western shirt looked like it had been through a hundred washings, and the heels of his boots bore signs of a hundred miles of wear and tear.

"Good morning." Chase stepped up onto the veranda and stretched out his hand. "I'm Chase Morgan."

The old man looked up at him with a squint to his eye. "Yup." He shook Chase's hand without breaking eye contact. "First name's Bull. Last name don't matter because it ain't shit."

Chase laughed and gave a nod to the I'M AN OLD FART. WHAT'S YOUR EXCUSE? coffee mug in the man's hand. "Got any more of that coffee?"

"Faith keeps a big pot brewin' all day in the kitchen. Tastes best when it gets to the bottom." He lifted the mug. "But this'll do. Go on in and help yourself."

With a thanks, Chase headed inside, stopping to look

at the now-fully-decorated tree and great room. Looked like Faith had stayed up all night to get the job done.

Regardless of his personal beliefs on the holiday, the room looked spectacular. Decked out in colors of rust red and gold, the decorations on the tree blended with the strings of gilded beads and white lights like the perfect notes of a symphony. Even the swag of evergreen across the front of the fireplace was lit up and adorned with gigantic red and gold jingle bells.

The sight took him back to the days when he, Boone, and Cassidy had stood side by side decorating a tree their daddy had brought home from a tree lot. They'd all go pick it out together and take a vote on which one made it to their living room. Chase had always felt bad when New Year's Day came and out went the tree without a single shimmery bauble or equal fanfare as to the way it had come in the house.

The memory squeezed his stomach. Before the misery could make its way into his throat, he went into the kitchen. There he found a woman as wide as she was tall in a long calico skirt and a Magic Box Ranch T-shirt stirring something in the pot on the stove that smelled like a slice of heaven with a dash of bacon. Her coppery hair fell into a long plait down the center of her back. When he entered the room, she turned toward him and flashed a grin across her broad face.

"You must be Mr. Morgan. I'm Shelby, the head cook." She wiped her palm on the plaid apron tied at her plump waist, then extended it to shake his hand. "We're so pleased you could join us. Would you like me to fix you up some breakfast? Maybe a nice omelet or a country scramble?"

"Call me Chase. And I don't want to be any trouble. I was actually just looking for a cup of coffee."

"Nonsense." She made her way over to a rolling cart that held a large Air Pot and all the fixings you could imagine for a cup of coffee. She grabbed a mug and pumped it full of a strong, steaming brew. "Faith would have my skin if I didn't see you got something to eat. Do you take cream or sugar?"

"Black's just fine." He took the cup and debated going back out onto the veranda to sit with Bull or staying right there with Shelby to see what she had cooking on the stove. "So, is Faith your boss?"

"I guess you could say that. Basically, we all work together as a group, but when it comes down to facts and figures, Faith is our girl."

Interesting.

"She said you helped her set up the tree last night," Shelby said. "We appreciate that. She tries to wrangle us in every year. But between decorating the lodge house, the barn, and our own homes, one tends to get a little burned-out on all the holly jolly, if you know what I mean."

"I do."

"Now, Faith?" Shelby smiled even as she shook her head. "She never gets tired of it. It's like she was born with mistletoe in her blood or something."

"She does seem to enjoy the process."

"Oh, it's not just the process or even just Christmas.

She puts every drop of her blood, sweat, and tears into this place. Sometimes we all just expect her to drop from pure exhaustion. Oddly, it seems to be the exhaustion she thrives on. Well, that and about a pot and a half of rich, dark brew."

Chase sipped his own coffee and nodded his approval. "It's very good."

"Sounds like you're not much of a breakfast person. Let me just whip you up something quick and light, and I'll bring it out to you in the dining room."

He didn't have the heart to tell her he wasn't hungry, so he just smiled, and said, "That sounds great. But I'd prefer to eat in here if you don't mind."

Shelby's copper eyebrows shot up. "In the kitchen?"

He nodded. "I'm not much of a fancy-dining-room kind of guy. I ate dinner in here last night with Faith."

"Well, don't that beat all." Shelby's fists went to a pair of wide hips. "It's not like her to allow guests to eat in the kitchen."

"Why not?"

"Oh, she's got this idea in that pretty head that the kitchen is sacred ground. You know, it's like the dividing line between the rich and the . . . well, you get my meaning."

"Sounds like Faith might be a bit of a snob."

"Oh! Not at all. It's just . . . there's a bit of history there that I'm not at liberty to share. If you stay around long enough, you can ask her yourself." She gave him a long once-over. "And if she let you in her kitchen, I'm guessing you'll be staying."

Faith was becoming more of a mystery than he'd ever imagined. He already knew she had a generous heart with her charity work. So what else dwelled beneath those nice, firm breasts and adorable dimples? What secrets was she harboring? And why did everyone make it sound like she ran the Magic Box Guest Ranch all on her own?

"How did you come to work at the ranch, Shelby?"

"Oh, guess you could say I'm a stray like all the rest. Husband left me a few years back with three little boys and no income. I got a job washing dishes at Bud's Diner in the mornings after I sent the kids to school. Paige—Faith's sister—gave Faith a call and told her all about me. Next thing I knew, Faith had come into Bud's for a burger and asked if I knew how to cook. The rest, as they say, is history."

"Sounds like Faith has a big heart."

"Now there's an understatement. When she found out me and my boys didn't have a place to hang our hats, she moved us into one of the bigger cabins until I could save up enough to find us a place of our own."

"So she's generous too."

Shelby nodded. "And smart as a whip."

Curiosity rolled into a big pile of "what if" inside his head. For a man who was always at the top of his game, the notion that he currently had more questions than answers didn't sit well.

"If it's all right with you," he said to Shelby, "I'll take that breakfast out on the veranda. There's a man named Bull out there who looks like he's full of good stories."

"That he is." She laughed. "He's full of something else

too. You go on and have yourself a sit. I'll be out in a jiffy with your meal."

WHEN FAITH PULLED the big ranch truck into the shade beside the barn, she spotted Chase sitting in the big red rocking chair on the veranda with a mug of coffee in his hand, smiling at some line Bull was feeding him. She didn't know why just the sight of Chase made her stomach quiver. Well, other than the fact that he was gorgeous.

Yeah, that would about do it.

Especially for a woman who'd gone so long without intimacy with a man she'd almost forgotten what it was all about.

Almost.

Last night, after falling into his arms, decorating the tree, then sharing a meal and laughter, her dreams had been filled with vivid, steamy reminders.

He looked different today. Less like he should be on a polo field—sipping mint juleps, not playing the game. Less like he should be rocking a three-piece suit and heading up a boardroom executive meeting.

Less . . . stuffy.

Maybe that had to do with the way his hair looked like he'd simply run his fingers through it after his morning shower rather than the careful way it had been combed when he'd arrived yesterday. Or maybe it had to do with the tight black T-shirt hugging his lean, sculpted muscles. Or maybe it was the pair of jeans he wore stacked over a dusty, worn pair of shitkickers.

Her eyes slammed back down to his big feet.

Where the heck had he gotten cowboy boots? And highly broken-in ones at that?

Arms loaded down with supplies to restock the refrigerator and to replace the icicle lights that had blown out this past year, she headed toward the men, who appeared to be having the time of their lives.

Odd, because Bull rarely smiled. He was a broken-down old cowboy who'd have been pulling himself from the gutter every day if she hadn't taken him in, changed his way of thinking, and given him a job. The loss of his wife four years ago had sent him to his knees, and he'd had a hard time getting back up. Lola Crothers had been the love of his life since they married at only sixteen years of age. Never having been gifted with children, they'd spent nearly seventy years side by side as lovers and best friends.

Until that fateful morning when Lola just didn't wake up.

Old Bull had wanted to crawl into that grave beside her. Instead, he'd crawled into a bottle. The only time he'd looked up was when Faith had offered him a friendly smile and a soft shoulder. From that moment, Bull had become family. But at the moment, she had to wonder exactly what he was up to.

"Hey there." Chase's cheery smile widened when he saw her although he didn't offer to get up out of that comfortable rocker and lend a hand with the packages.

"I was just sitting here talking with Bull," Chase said. "And guess what he just told me?"

"That a Southern gentleman offers to help a lady with her burden?"

"Not even close." Chase clapped Bull's bony shoulder in a "Hey, Buddy" gesture. "Bull here? He just told me that you don't just *work* here at the Magic Box Ranch. You actually *own* the place."

Faith flashed a glare at Bull, who didn't even bother to appear apologetic. Had she thought Bull was family? At the moment, he seemed to fit well in the wicked-stepsister department.

"Is that so?" She tilted her head to take the shine off Chase's toothy grin. "And why would you even be interested in such a matter, Mr. Morgan?"

"Sweet thing." Chase stood and pressed a knee against the chair to keep it from rocking. Apparently, he too believed the old wives' tale that it was bad luck to let an empty rocker rock. "When it comes to you . . . I've got interest a mile long."

He came toward her with a confident swagger and, unsure of his intent, she took a step back.

"Give me the bags, Faith." He held out his hands. "Then how about you and I have a little . . . chat?"

Faith gave up the grocery bags. Tossed Bull a "We will discuss this later" scowl. And spit fire as she followed Chase into the house.

"BULL HAD NO business giving you that information."

Chase kept the smile from his face as Faith followed

him into the kitchen. As he set the bags on the counter, he could feel the heat of her ire singeing his backside.

Catching the drift that something was amiss, Shelby put down the big wooden spoon she'd been using to stir whatever was in the huge, cast-iron Dutch oven that smelled so delicious and made a quick exit.

When Chase and Faith were alone, he turned and noted a flush highlighting her cheeks that he'd guess had nothing to do with the room temperature. He leaned back against the counter, folded his arms, and cocked one ankle over the other. "Soooo . . . why the big secret?"

Pretty hands slammed down on shapely hips. "Aren't you supposed to be relaxing and getting the stink of the city off you by doing ridiculous things like demanding expensive bottles of champagne or a hot-stone massage from a Barbie-doll blonde?"

"You do hot-stone massages here?"

"Don't try to be sneaky and change the subject. And why are you dressed like . . ." Her hand fluttered. "That?"

"I didn't think helping out around here would work very well if I was wearing Armani."

"And why would you want to help out around here? You're on a sabbatical. You're a paying customer. Remember?"

"Why the big secret, Faith?" He pushed away from the counter and moved toward her. When she didn't back away from his advance, he smiled. He liked a woman who wasn't afraid of a challenge. And he liked knowing that

Faith didn't see him as any kind of threat. Although if she could read his mind, she'd be looking for something to cover up that lusciously female body.

He came to a halt right in front of her. Close enough to reach out, cup her lovely face, and lower his head to kiss her plump, soft lips. Somehow, he refrained from doing just that. "Why don't you want anyone to know you're the owner of the Magic Box Ranch?"

She snagged her bottom lip between her teeth and gave his inquiry a good amount of consideration before she responded. Her response could be anything from a lie, to the truth, to telling him it was none of his damn business. He kept his fingers crossed for honesty. And because she was a woman who always seemed to tell the truth no matter how uncomfortable it might be, he had no doubt her response would be as from the heart as anything else she did.

"When Paige and I were teenagers, our uncle Charles would hire us to come help him on the ranch. While our girlfriends were hanging around Pop's Soda Shop, hungry for a date, we'd be working our tails off pushing steers and shoveling manure. Back then, it was just a cattle ranch. But my uncle paid us well, and I saved up the money to go to college. After I graduated, I worked as a rehabilitation therapist at Memorial Hermann in Houston. When my uncle Charles became ill, I quit my job and came home so I could help him out. When he passed away, I found out he'd left me the ranch."

Her shoulders came up in a shrug. "Guess I saw more

in this old place than he ever did, so I started working toward making it what it is today."

"Admirable."

"If you say so."

"I do. But that doesn't answer my question."

She gave him a direct look with those smoky eyes. "The reason I don't tell guests I'm the owner is because men of a certain status—at least the ones who pay a healthy fee to come here—don't seem to have much respect for a *girl* trying to build a dream."

"What do you mean not much respect?" A hundred images flew into Chase's head—each one worse than the rest—that made him hope he wouldn't have to go hunt someone down for hurting her.

"I'm not talking about anything physical, so just get that *ready to kick some ass* look out of your eye. I just mean that they have a tendency to laugh. They find it hard to believe a simple backwoods girl like me—who wears jeans and boots—could achieve something this big. It's just disrespectful. I graduated summa cum laude from the University of Houston, for Pete's sake."

There seemed to be no end to the surprises hidden in the very lovely package that was Faith Walker.

"So how do you deal with it," he asked. "Other than hide the information?"

A smirk kissed her lips. "Oh, you know . . . silly, immature things like putting them on the orneriest horse in the corral. Or telling them that the Perrier-Jouët they ordered wouldn't arrive in time for their massage appointment. Just little things that would tick them off in big ways."

He laughed. "You have a lot of spunk."

"I'm not sure I'd call it that. Low tolerance for wealthy jerks who like to throw their status around would probably be a better description."

Ouch.

"Who wounded you, Faith?"

"Wounded me?" Her head tilted, just slightly. But Chase had been in enough heated boardroom discussions to recognize that no matter the expression on a person's face, the movement was a sign of affirmation.

"Yes. What *wealthy* man tried to steal your fire? Wounded your soul? Left you so broken inside that *you've* become the snob?"

Those dark gray eyes flashed just before they narrowed. "Excuse me?"

"I've been here less than twenty-four hours, and not once, not twice, but more than a handful of times you've expressed your displeasure with the upper echelon of financially comfortable society. You even lumped me in with the bunch though you really know nothing about me, what I do for a living, or even how hard I work."

He paused. Waited for her to deny his accusations. She surprised him by remaining silent.

"So tell me. Why did you quit your job and leave Houston? Was it just because your uncle was ill? Or were you fleeing something—or someone—unpleasant?"

Her breasts lifted on one deep breath. Then two.

"A woman doesn't usually walk away from a job she loves or has worked hard to obtain," she said. "It was about a man. As pathetic as that sounds."

"And in this case the man was . . . ?"

"My fiancé. I won't repeat his name for fear the earth will split wide open and swallow me up because I swore I'd never utter his name again."

So honest. Chase admired the hell out of that. He offered a grim nod even though he'd rather have smiled. "And . . ."

"And, he was the head of orthopedic surgery and a bit older than me. I admired the way he treated his patients and how he worked so hard to find life-changing solutions for those who might otherwise have been forced to use wheelchairs. Like our soldiers who'd returned from war busted up by shrapnel from an IED and figured they'd live the rest of their lives in painful agony."

She glanced away but not to swipe away tears. The brief moment was clearly so she could rein in the resentment she still maintained.

"I thought we had so much in common," she continued, bringing her direct gaze back to him. "A passion for healing, family, and old-fashioned values. As you can imagine, as the head of orthopedic surgery, he lived well. Attended the kinds of events you see in the society pages of the newspaper. He treated me like a queen. For a girl who'd grown up without much and busted her ass and worked hard all her life, I'll admit, I liked being regarded and accepted by *that* side of the social order. He never made me feel like I didn't belong. I thought he was perfect. Right up to the day my uncle got sick and I wanted to come take care of him and the ranch."

"And your fiancé didn't approve?"

"*Ex*-fiancé. At first, he didn't mind that I came for a few weeks. But after my uncle died, and I discovered he'd left me the ranch, I wanted to stay. I thought maybe he'd see how important maintaining my uncle's dream meant to me. How much I had loved this place ever since I was a child. Like a fool, I thought he might consider accepting a position at a hospital in San Antonio or Austin. He was always getting offers, so I didn't think it was any big deal."

"And he proved you wrong?"

"Boy, did he." She shook her head. "I believe his exact words were, "I can't believe I wasted so much time trying to train you to be a member of the upper class. All you really are is a hillbilly who should never have left the farm.""

Chase stood speechless. Even as he watched the visible tension constrict her neck and jaw muscles. Even as she transferred her weight from one foot to the other and clenched her fists. The laugh that left her pretty mouth held anything but humor.

"I mean, really," she said, her wild hand gestures doing most of the talking for her. "We don't have *farms* in Texas. We have *ranches*. Big effing ranches that offer opportunities for underprivileged children to forget their troubles for a while. To dream big and discover they can be whatever the heck they want to be. Even a freaking hillbilly with a bachelor of science degree. So while he started out treating me like a queen, he ended up treating me like trash."

Bastard.

"So you're going to blame everyone else for one asshole's actions?"

She blinked. "I don't mean to."

"Anger and regret are a waste of energy, Faith." He knew a little about the power of those emotions. He'd spent an entire week reacting in the same way after his heart had stopped and changed his entire life.

The two of them had a lot in common. She'd loved her uncle and wanted to maintain his dream, much as he had with his father.

The difference?

She'd been brave enough to stay put. He'd run like a coward.

"Anger and regret don't change anything," he said. "Haven't you ever heard the saying, 'the best revenge is to live well and be happy'?"

"You're not at all who I think you are," she said, her eyes squinting. "Are you?"

"I hope not."

For a long moment, they stood there, gazes locked, the air around them thickening.

He took that last step closer to her. Simply because he couldn't have stopped himself if he'd tried.

Then he did exactly what he'd promised himself he wouldn't do. He reached out his hand and gently cupped her cheek. Her thick, dark lashes fluttered as she looked up at him. But she did not pull away. Unable to fight the desire burning through his blood, he lowered his head and pressed his lips to hers.

To his surprise and absolute satisfaction, she slid her

hands up his chest, wrapped her lovely arms around his neck, and leaned into his kiss.

As she lifted to her toes, her full breasts pressed into his chest, and a hot zap of lust spiked deep in his groin. His arms went around her, pulling her closer just as her moist mouth parted and let him in.

When their tongues met, a surge of pleasure so different from anything he'd ever felt before lit him up inside. Kissing Faith was like the Fourth of July and Christmas morning all rolled into one. In the warm recess of her mouth, their tongues tangled, danced, and made love. Chase could have stood there all day, holding her in his arms, kissing her until she moaned with the need of something more.

When she did just that, he gathered his wits and ended the kiss by once more pressing his mouth to the center of her luscious lips, then one to her forehead.

With a sigh, she stepped away, and his arms were instantly void of the pleasure of her warmth.

"Why did you kiss me?" she asked.

"Because I wanted to. Why did you kiss me back?"

She grinned. "Because I wanted to."

He returned the gesture. "Then we'd better be prepared. Because I'm guessing there are probably more where that one came from."

She flashed a come-and-get-me grin as she spun on the heels of those worn-down boots, and said, "A girl can only hope."

Chapter Four

THE DAY AFTER their breath-stealing, heart-pounding kiss, Chase disappeared. For, at last count, two days without a word as to where he was going.

Not that he owed her an explanation.

But hauling ass out of Dodge wasn't exactly the response a girl was looking for after she'd thrown caution to the wind and locked lips with a man she'd met only twenty-four hours earlier. Well, maybe she didn't exactly know him, but based on the way he handled himself, she had a pretty good idea who he *might* be. Either that, or she'd been watching way too many romantic comedies.

The second day of his disappearance, Faith began to wonder if he would come back at all or if she'd scared him away for good. Kissing a guest was bad for business. Not that she'd made the first move that day in the kitchen. But she had responded like he'd been a bowl of her favorite ice cream on a hot summer day.

She didn't know what had really brought him all the way to the Magic Box Guest Ranch because he hadn't given her that information. Neither had his cousin Abby. So maybe she should pull her head out of the south end of her body and pay attention to the warning signs. Maybe his being so secretive about his reasons for picking up and running from whatever was back in New York said a lot more about him than just a really hot kiss.

In fact, she was pretty danged sure it did.

Yet she couldn't dismiss the way he had kissed her.

Hot, hungry, yet restrained at the same time. His hands hadn't wandered all over her body. Just the same, the urgency in his touch told her he'd have been happy to remove her clothes and give her what she'd been missing for a really long time.

Passion.

Something about Chase Morgan said the man had a sincere appetite for life and appreciated the opposite sex. And she was a woman who'd been too long without that particular emotion for a man. Which was probably the only reason she was so intrigued.

Yeah. She'd go with that pathetic excuse.

Because at the end of the day, she saw good-looking men all the time. Texas overflowed with them. Heck, just down the road were the pinup boys of good-looking men who went by the last name of Wilder. So even though Chase Morgan fell in the upper level of manly hotness, it wasn't just his looks–or his body–that attracted her. It was something she couldn't quite put her finger on. Sure as Christmas was getting closer every day, Faith was drawn to him.

On the third day of his disappearance, she gave in to all the curiosity playing hide-and-seek in her brain and checked his cabin. Using the excuse that it was close to Christmas and Maria, the full-time housekeeper should be spending her time with her family rather than coming all the way to the ranch to clean just one cabin, Faith put her supersnooper sensors in gear and opened the unlocked door.

If he had been worried about privacy, he would have locked the door, right?

The warm and welcome scent of cinnamon sticks and crisp red apples greeted her as she stepped inside and found the cabin as neat as if no one had been staying there. Everything was in its place. Bed made. No dishes in the sink. Curtains open. The only sign that the cabin had recently been inhabited was a single coffee cup on the counter–rinsed and turned upside down to drain.

In all her thirty-two years, she'd never seen such a tidy man. Maybe all he needed was a little messing up. She thought of her own cluttered room back in the lodge house. Or maybe she could stand to take a few housekeeping lessons from him.

The large armoire against the far wall near the corner where she'd set up the small Christmas tree served as the cabin's closet and dresser. Her heels tapped on the floor as she crossed the room and pulled open the double doors.

Inside the cedar cabinet were shirts and pants neatly hung on wooden hangers. In the drawers were pristinely folded boxer briefs in colors of gray, blue, and black. Sharing drawer space were several black, blue, and white T-shirts.

Apparently, Chase had a thing for dark colors.

Lucky for him he looked amazing in them.

Maybe all he really needed was a little color in his life. Maybe that's why he'd come to Texas. Everyone knew the Lone Star State was a colorful place. Most believed God made Texas on his day off just for sheer entertainment. There were even folks who swore they'd rather be a fencepost in Texas than king of the world. So maybe all Chase really had in mind was a little distraction from the mad rush of New York. Maybe all he really had in mind was a little Southern hospitality and a good time.

Questions were: Where the heck had he gone for three whole days? And did *she* intend to be his good time?

Faith closed the drawers, then turned back to face the empty room. Only it wasn't quite as empty as it had been when she'd first come through the door.

"Snooping, Faith?" Chase's muscular silhouette loomed large in the open doorway. His deep voice was tinged with humor. "You're such an openly honest woman, it hardly seems your style."

"Disappearing for three days without a word might be *your* style," she said, trying to keep the mortification from getting busted from her voice. "But *I* have a business to run. And I needed to know whether you were coming back or not in case someone else wanted to rent this cabin."

"I prepaid for the entire ten days."

"Yes. Well, I would have refunded your money if you hadn't come back."

"Uh-huh." When he came into the room and walked right up to her, she noticed the hint of amusement playing at the corners of his masculine lips. "Thought you said you didn't rent out cabins this time of year."

"I don't, but–"

"You were snooping, Faith. Admit it. It's not the end of the world."

"Okay. Fine." A hard breath whooshed from her lungs. "I was snooping."

The quirk of his smile went full tilt. "Find anything interesting?"

"You're a neat freak. And you only wear dark colors. And I no longer need to wonder boxers or briefs."

His dark brows shot up his forehead. "And that's interesting how?"

She shrugged. "Okay, so maybe it's not as interesting as it is curiosity-satisfying."

"You were curious about the kind of underwear I put on?" He folded his arms beneath the pair of aviator sunglasses hanging from the crew neck of the black T-shirt stretched tight across his fabulously defined pecs, abdomen, and narrow waist. Chase was long and lean, with a physique that appeared to be more from living a healthy lifestyle and long-distance running than the men she saw posing on the Internet like a bunch of muscle-bound Arnold Schwarzeneggers. Not that she hunted up photos of muscle men on Google . . . too frequently.

Because it was actually the curiosity of what Chase would look like when he took off that butt-hugging underwear that bothered her, she realized she needed to escape this whole fiasco of a conversation.

"Sorry I snooped." She stepped around him and headed toward the door. He was fast and caught her by the arm.

"Running doesn't seem your style, either." He smirked like he knew she was running from him.

She wasn't. Exactly. She was really running from the way he made her feel and the sensations he awakened inside her. Maybe she was just afraid she might do something stupid and unforgivable, like push him down on that big king-sized bed, tear his clothes off, and climb on top.

God, her fantasies were out of control. She had to get a life.

The knowing smile he flashed verified it.

CHASE COULDN'T HELP but grin when Faith's eyes revealed the truth.

She was running, but not from him. She was running from herself and the way they'd heated up that kitchen three days ago.

Rightly so that she seemed agitated when he'd disappeared without telling her or anyone where he was going or if he'd even come back.

In truth, he'd given in to the guilt that had weighed heavy in his chest for years, and he'd returned to Stephenville to visit Boone and Cassidy at the longhorn ranch where he'd been raised. Driving the Chevy Silverado half-ton he'd rented in San Antonio, he'd gone through almost four hours of flatlands before he finally saw familiar landmarks like the Lone Star Arena and Moola, the cow statue in front of the county courthouse.

The more miles he'd put on the truck, the more he'd been surprised to sense the undeniable pull toward the small Texas town. Or maybe it had just been the eagerness to see Boone and Cassidy again. His enthusiasm had died, however, when he pulled up in front of the ranch-style house and parked. Memories flooded him, and he'd almost turned the key in the ignition and driven off. But then his little sister, now a lovely, full-grown woman, had pushed open the screen door and, long dark hair flying, raced across the drive and launched herself into his arms.

Boone had followed up with a bear hug and a slap on the back. From there, Chase finally found the courage to take a deep breath and step inside the house.

On a mighty exhale, he realized that everything had changed. The color of the walls. The furniture. The kitchen layout. Even the pencil markings that recorded his, Boone, and Cassidy's growth on the inside of the hall closet door were gone. The entire country vibe of the four-bedroom house had been transformed into something trendy and modern.

Relief freed the boulder from his chest. He didn't know what he'd expected to see after all these years, but he'd been thankful his fears had been for naught. The memories of his dad would remain in his heart, not as a ghost sitting in his old leather recliner.

The visit had gone so well he'd stayed longer than he'd originally planned. He'd been invited to stay for Christmas, but even with as well as things had gone, even with all the physical changes within those walls, he knew he could not be in that house on that day. Before he'd driven off to head back to the Magic Box Guest Ranch, his brother and sister told him anytime he wanted to come back home, they'd be there with open arms.

Going back had been a huge step. But he wasn't ready for any long-term commitments to anything.

Not yet.

Not until he'd come to terms with the radical change in his life. A change that left him unsure of the direction he'd go after these ten days at the Magic Box Ranch. Ten days that surely promised to intensify his attraction to the ranch's sexy owner.

Regardless of what her jackass of an ex-fiancé had done, Faith was the kind of woman a man didn't take for granted. She was the kind of woman a man protected, spoiled, and loved for the rest of his life.

He didn't know if he could ever be that man for Faith or any woman. It wasn't because he didn't believe in love or long-term relationships. It was simply because he didn't know who the hell he was anymore. Everything he'd planned for his life had disintegrated with one skipped heartbeat.

How could he ever pledge his life to a woman when

he didn't know a damned thing about the life he lived anymore?

What did the future hold for him?

What would he do?

Where would he go?

A woman like Faith needed a stable man who had his shit together and knew exactly what he wanted in life.

He was lost.

But even that didn't stop him from wanting her.

"I'm not running," she said. The determination tightening her lips didn't make it any less a lie. "There are only two more weeks till the charity event, and I have work to do." She untangled her arm from his grasp. "You, however, as a paying guest, have many choices."

"Such as?"

"Well, you can take a hike."

He laughed. "Literally?"

"Funny." She wrinkled her nose. "We have several lovely hiking trails that follow the banks of the creek. Most of the trails are beneath a canopy of trees, so you don't need to worry about heatstroke."

About the only stroke he was bound to have was because of the way she filled out a pair of jeans and that Magic Box Ranch T-shirt.

"Or you can check with Bull," she said, stealthily easing toward the door like he wouldn't notice. "I'm sure he'd be happy to take you on a ride. Most of our horses are well broke for inexperienced riders. Or you can grab a pole and go down to the fishing pond. It's stocked with some smallmouth bass and catfish. Or I can schedule you for a hot-stone massage. Or–"

"Are you the massage therapist?"

Her eyes widened. "No."

"Too bad."

She cleared her throat and took a step backward. "Or if you feel like playing a game of chess, Bull would probably be up for that too."

"Long list."

"We try to satisfy everyone's needs."

Now didn't that just shoot a whole bunch of interesting images through his imagination.

"I've made my choice," he said.

"Great." She gave him a relieved smile. "What will it be so I can contact the right person to help you?"

"I'm going to help *you*."

She gave him an obstinate lift of her chin. "That wasn't an option."

"It is now."

Chapter Five

THE FOLLOWING NIGHT, Faith realized she hadn't been very good at keeping her distance from the paying guest. She hadn't been very good at keeping her eyes off him. And she hadn't been very good at keeping her imagination from wandering like a cat in heat down a back alley.

True to his word, yesterday afternoon, he'd followed her into the barn and helped her work on the decorations for the charity barn dance. Although his choices of helping and his methods of doing so had left her more than a little flustered.

When she'd climbed the ladder to hang the strings of twinkling lights and the shimmery gold and silver stars, he held her by the waist instead of holding the ladder. When she went to arrange the decorated garlands along the tops of the stalls, he held her up so she "didn't have to bother" getting the stepstool. He used every reason possible to touch her.

And she'd let him.

God, she was pathetic.

Sure, she'd been grateful for the help. But along with the help came a heavy dose of becoming more familiar with the man. The only thing she hadn't gotten to know was where he'd been for three days. The curiosity was killing her. Maybe he'd gone to see a woman. He did seem a little more relaxed when he'd come back. Maybe Faith was making a total fool of herself. Maybe she should just knock him on his very attractive behind and tell him to keep his hands to himself.

Only one thing she knew for certain.

These days, a whole lot of maybes floated into her head that had no place being there.

"I can't help but notice how y'all know your way around a horse pretty well," Faith said as they rode toward the patch of evergreens where she planned to snip some fresh bundles for the barn decorations.

Over breakfast, he'd talked her into letting him come along, then he followed her into the stables. She'd expected him to stand in the doorway and watch her saddle the horses. Instead, he'd strolled past the stalls, checking out each animal as though he were looking to purchase a thoroughbred fit to win the Kentucky Derby. When she went to saddle Rainbow for him, one of their gentlest quarter horse mares, Chase shook his head and pointed toward Zip, the orneriest gelding on the ranch. Usually, Faith or Bull rode the sleek buckskin. But Chase insisted.

Imagining a lawsuit that would pitch her headfirst into the red zone of her financial spreadsheets, she reluctantly gave in to the man's wishes. Surprise filled every pore in her body when he'd lifted the pad and saddle off the stand, easily slung it over Zip's back, then proceeded to pull up the cinch strap and put on the bridle just as though he'd done it every day of his life. He even cleaned Zip's hooves like a pro.

Faith had watched him with her arms folded and her suspicion increasing by the minute.

"I might have ridden a horse a time or two in my day," he said, tucking the bill of the New York Rangers cap lower over his expressive green eyes.

"Just like you might have worn stacked Wranglers and boots before?"

A smirk tilted those sizzling man lips. "Maybe."

Since they'd kissed, she'd tried to ignore that funny little flutter in her heart that said Chase Morgan wasn't just your average high-dollar-earning executive or just a great kisser.

Well, he was that.

On second thought, she'd take that back.

The man wasn't just a great kisser; he kissed like he meant it. Like she was the only woman in the world, and he wanted to focus on all the details that would make her moan, scream out loud, and beg for more.

She'd surprised herself by walking right into that kiss. It had been a long time since she'd been held in a man's arms. A long time since she'd felt the sensuous pressure of a man's mouth on hers. A long time since she'd had that uncontrollable urge to rip off her clothes and jump his incredibly hot body right there in the middle of the kitchen, where anyone could have walked in and caught them.

"Mmmhmm." She tore her gaze from the way he sat a saddle like he'd been born to it and focused across the field toward their destination. "Well, you might have *walking* that horse down to an art. But let's see how good you can really ride."

With a "Ha!" she kicked Rainbow into a full gallop. Chase not only followed and kept up, he handled Zip with a level of expertise that proved he was full of baloney with his big-city-boy game.

She beat him by a split second and only because she knew the hidden pitfalls to avoid while flying across that field. Rainbow had barely come to a halt before she was off the saddle and charging toward Chase.

"Who the hell are you?" she demanded. "No suit-wearing ad exec from Manhattan rides like that!"

"Damn that was exhilarating." He came off Zip's back with ease, then towered over her with a grin. "Watch where you're pointing that finger, sweet thing."

She retracted her pointer, then slammed her hands down on her hips. "No more BS, Chase. Who the hell are you?"

He took a step toward her. Then another. Stubborn from the day she was born, she stayed planted. Even as the seductive look in his eyes kicked her heart into overdrive.

"I . . ." His big hands slid gently over the slope of her shoulders. "Am the man who's going to kiss you. Right now. Not just because I've got too much exhilaration racing through me. But because every time I look at you, I just feel like smiling. And doing this."

Before she could protest—which hadn't even entered her mind—Chase pulled her into his arms and pressed his mouth to hers like she was the most important thing in his world, and he hadn't seen her in forever.

His tongue slicked across the seam of her lips, teased, and urged her to let him in. Since her mama didn't raise no fools, she gave in and let the firestorm of sensation rushing through her veins roar over reason.

IN THE GRAND scheme of things, Chase hadn't planned to kiss her. But now that his lips were on hers, and she was warm and supple in his arms, he was glad for the impulsive act. As he ended the kiss, lifted his head, and looked into her inquisitive eyes, reality slammed down.

The trip home to Stephenville had given him the first inkling that he was on some kind of path toward his future. He didn't know yet what that might be, but the kiss he'd just shared with Faith confirmed that there was something leading him. He had a strong feeling that something was his heart—an organ in his body he'd ignored physically and emotionally until just a few weeks ago.

"Not going to apologize for that," he said. "If you didn't like it, slap me, belt me, or do something, so I don't do it again."

Those pretty lips of hers pursed like she was trying to disconnect her mouth from her brain. Or her heart.

"I never said I didn't like it."

Lucky for him, Faith was the kind of woman who always said what she was thinking.

Her lashes swept down in a long blink. "I just want to know who I'm kissing."

"How about we go cut those evergreens you came here for?"

"How about you cut the crap and tell me who you are? Why is it such a big secret? Are you hiding out from the FBI or something? Maybe you're a serial killer. Should I be getting on my horse and riding away from you as fast as I can go?"

"Probably." He chuckled. Not only was she honest, she jumped to big conclusions. "Don't worry. I'm not dangerous."

"Says who?"

He kissed her again just because he had to. "Does that taste like danger to you?"

"Yes." She pushed him away and headed toward her horse. "A kiss tells me nothing. Women fall in love with mass murderers behind bars all the time. While *they* might be certifiably crazy, *I* am not."

He caught up to her just before she set her foot in the stirrup and took her by the arm. "I promise. I'm not Charles Manson or anything like him."

"Then why won't you tell me who you are?" The concern pulling her delicately arched brows together tugged at his heart.

How did he tell this woman, who in just a few short days had come to mean something to him, about all the things that had happened in the past few weeks? How did he explain the series of events that had changed his life and how now he didn't have any idea in which direction he was headed? How did he wash away the deep-seated fear that if he told her he had a heart condition, she might run?

He didn't want Faith to run anywhere except straight into his arms.

"Let's get out of the sun. And I'll explain." He took her by the arm and led her beneath the thick canopy of oaks. Even in the winter, the Texas sun could get hotter than hell.

She followed him, boots scuffing in the dry earth. When they got beneath the trees, she sat down on one of the large mounds of tree roots, folded her hands in her lap, and waited.

Pacing, he rubbed his chin.

Where to start?

"A couple of weeks ago, I made the decision to leave my position at the advertising agency I've worked at for almost ten years."

"Why?"

Truth?

Yes.

"Because I almost died. I'm only thirty-four, and when I realized the stress of the job would most likely kill me, I thought of all the things I'd be missing."

"You almost died?" Her eyes widened and he waited for her to run. "How?"

"Stress-related heart attack."

In his head, he counted the tense silent seconds that passed between them. In the next breath, she was off that tree root and enveloping him in her arms. Her warmth filled something in his soul he hadn't even realized he'd been missing.

"Oh, Chase. I'm so sorry. I had no idea." She looked up at him, apology burning in the depth of her eyes. "I'm sorry I pushed you. It's really none of my business."

"It's just not easy to tell a woman you're interested in that for the first time in your life, you're wandering aimlessly without a plan for your future. I thought I had it all figured out from the time I was a kid pushing longhorns on my daddy's ranch in Stephenville."

"Stephenville! That's the Cowboy Capital of the World." She smiled. "So you *do* know a thing or two about horses."

"And cattle. The other day, I went to see my brother and sister, who run the ranch. I haven't been back for years. After our father died, we all bought the ranch as a partnership so our remarried mother could move on with her life. It was just too hard to let all my daddy's dreams be sold off."

"So that's where you went when you disappeared? You went home?"

He nodded, loving the way she stayed in his arms as they talked. "When I was eighteen, my dad died of a heart attack on Christmas morning. I haven't been back since."

"Christmas!" She hugged him again. "Oh, Chase, I'm so sorry. That must have been so hard for you."

"Still is." He stroked his hands up and down her back.

"I'll admit I haven't been overly fond of the holiday since then."

Sadness darkened her eyes. "And here I've had you putting up decorations and practically forcing you to find your holiday cheer."

He shrugged. "I've been happy to help."

"Liar." Her smile took the sting off the accusation. "Tell me about your dad."

"He was only forty-two and a hardworking man who loved his family. He taught me everything I know about ranching. But after he died, I didn't want to end up like him, in an early grave. So I chose a different path. Ironic, right?"

"And scary."

He decided to leave out the part about the ex-girlfriend running out on him. Not because he had any less fear about a repeat but because he could hardly compare an honorable woman like Faith to someone like her.

"When Abby found out about my heart attack, she called me and talked me into coming here for a much-needed break. But it's been more like facing my demons."

"What's your prognosis?"

He shrugged. "No damage. No lasting effects. Doctors couldn't even pinpoint why it had happened except that it was most likely stress-related. I decided the path I'd chosen for my life probably wasn't the right one for me anymore."

"What is?"

"I'm not sure." He pulled her in closer. "But right now I'm pretty glad Abby made that call."

"Me too." Her smile lit him up inside as she lifted to the toes of her boots, curled her arms around his neck, and pressed her sweet lips to his.

Stolen kisses were one thing.

But a kiss freely given by someone you'd just dared to trust with your heart meant everything.

Chapter Six

IT WAS A no-brainer for Chase to extend his stay at the Magic Box Guest Ranch. And the extension had nothing to do with having nowhere to go. He could find someplace easy enough. He just didn't want to leave. There was one thing keeping his boots firmly in place.

And her name was Faith.

Two weeks passed, with more projects on the ranch than he'd had ever seen on his desk in New York. When it came to planning the Christmas holiday and her charity event, Faith was an F5 Texas tornado. For the first time in his life, he had an opportunity to see the other side of life, like making lists and checking them twice, excusing the naughty and making sure the nice were rewarded, and shopping, and decorating, and meeting the good folks of Sweet, who couldn't seem to lend a helping hand fast enough. Minute by minute, he began to see the Christmas celebration through different eyes. Hers.

This time of year meant something to her. It was special. And as much as he tried to fight her infectious enthusiasm, he found he could not.

When he'd escorted Faith on the trips into the charming little town of Sweet to buy supplies, he noticed how much people liked her. He had to admit he fell into that category too.

At night, when they finished marking off each chore on her list, they sat together at the kitchen table and ate the delicious dinners Shelby had prepared for them. They laughed, talked, and got to know each other. They'd fallen into a routine of sharing coffee in the morning, a trail ride in the afternoons, and once Faith locked the doors to the business, they sat on the sofa with the lights twinkling on the tree, a fire crackling in the fireplace, and traditional Christmas tunes creating the spirit of the holiday Chase hadn't dared enjoy since that fateful holiday so long ago.

He thought back to all the beautiful wintry sights he'd seen in Manhattan. Central Park was gorgeous in the snow. The window displays at Macy's, Saks Fifth Avenue, and Bloomingdale's were elegant and inspiring. But not a single one of them compared to the warm Texas days he'd been sharing with Faith.

He'd *never* cuddled with anyone in his entire adult life.

Cuddling with Faith was like a zen experience. An addiction. He couldn't get enough. Yet for the first time since he'd first noticed the opposite sex all those adolescent years ago, he didn't feel like pushing to hurry up and get to the reward. He was willing to sit back and let things fall in place like a jigsaw puzzle that, once all the individual pieces fit together, would become a beautiful picture.

Maybe the whole near-death experience had ripped away his man card and turned him into a big pansy-ass. But he didn't think so. The power of these newfound feelings had the ability to reach out and show him the things that were truly important in life.

Family.

Friends.

A woman to love and cherish.

Which was why, as he and Faith cuddled on the sofa, he'd occasionally tear his gaze off her beautiful face and look way up at that big damn Christmas tree he'd helped her decorate. Against anything he ever believed he'd do, he'd find himself wishing on that shiny tin star at the very top. The one she'd been trying to position all alone, then fallen into his arms.

What would have happened had he not been here that night? The thought shuddered through him.

He'd been given the opportunity for a second chance. A new life. He didn't need a big red bow or fancy wrappings to recognize a gift when he found one.

Tonight, with her charity Christmas barn dance in full swing, the evergreen twinkling, the stars shining, and the mood glittering, he glanced across the barn to where Faith stood talking to a couple of elderly ladies he'd been introduced to earlier. On the surface, Gladys Lewis and Arlene Potter appeared to be your typical Golden Girl types—sweet, a little gossipy, with wholesome hearts. They'd blown that image to smithereens a few minutes ago when they'd trapped him near the punch bowl. He was pretty sure they'd passed the *cougar* stage, but apparently that wasn't going to stop them from putting on the big flirt.

"So how do you like our Faith?" Aiden Marshall, Faith's brother-in-law, extended his hand. They'd met a few days before, and Chase instantly appreciated the former Army Ranger's integrity, heart, and honor. He was watching out for Faith, and Chase couldn't blame him.

"I like her quite well."

"You've been watching her all night." Aiden's eyes flashed. "Giving her looks that say there's something more than *quite well*."

Chase shrugged. "Might be."

"She's special," Aiden said. "Just like her sister. You keep that in mind."

"Absolutely."

With a nod, Aiden walked off and joined his pretty wife at the silent-auction table. Seconds later, Chase was joined by a small woman with big blond hair.

"I'm Jana Wilder." Instead of extending her hand, she pulled him in for a hug. "You probably don't remember me, sugarplum, but we met when you were here visiting Abby and her family one summer. I think you might have been around eight years old."

"I apologize. I don't remember."

"Oh." Jana waved her hand. "Doesn't really matter. But you sure were a cute little thing back in the day. Looks like you've grown up in a good way."

He laughed. Nothing like good old honesty. No wonder Faith excelled in that area. She surrounded herself with the same down-to-earth type of people.

"You know, your cousin Abby is about to become my daughter-in-law," Jana said.

"So I heard. And after meeting you, I have trust your son will treat her well."

"Aren't you sweet." She patted his cheek. "We do like our weddings around here. The more the merrier. Just sayin'."

Before Chase could delve deeper into the meaning of her remark, she whipped her head around, and said, "Huh. Will you look at that. Old Chester Banks is dancin' with Gertie West. I'd best go make sure he doesn't step on her toes. They're arthritic, you know."

Chase didn't know, but he figured Jana's excuse to escape was probably the most original he'd heard all night.

He'd barely taken a breath, folded his arms, and leaned back against a horse-stall post to watch Faith across the room in her white lace dress, denim jacket, and boots. She'd left her long hair down tonight, and it curled prettily around her face. And while she looked sweet as country pie, he was getting hot and bothered.

The lace dress she wore had a row of buttons all the way down the front from the scooped neckline that revealed a hint of cleavage to the frilly hem that hit just above her knee. He couldn't stop thinking about slowly undoing all those buttons and unwrapping her like a present. He thought of running his hands through all that soft, silky hair and pulling her bare, shapely legs around his waist.

"She doesn't have a brother, but I'm willing to wipe that look off your face real fast."

Chase's head snapped around, and his attention immediately focused on the three big men surrounding him like a pack of wolves.

"You mind giving me your name first, so I'll know who's kicking my ass?"

"Jackson Wilder. These are my brothers Reno and Jesse."

"I don't suppose you'd like an explanation of what I was looking at?"

"Nope." Jesse Wilder stepped in and thrust out his hand while Reno stood back and grinned. "If you knew us any better, you'd know why."

Chase shook the extended hand, then the rest that came his way.

"We've been in your shoes," Reno said. "Know what you're thinking. Just be careful. Faith is like family."

Chase nodded. They weren't the first to warn him off tonight, but when Jackson said, "*If* you're still around after Christmas, we'll buy you a beer at Seven Devils' Saloon," Chase figured the warnings held little bite.

"Sounds great."

As the trio walked away, Chase laughed. It was nice to know so many people had Faith's back. But they didn't need to worry about him breaking her heart.

He, unfortunately, couldn't say the same for her.

FAITH HAD DONE her work, and now the payoff would come through the generosity of her friends and the community.

While the sweet scent of fresh evergreen boughs and warm apple cider wafted deliciously through the barn, the kindergartners from Sweet Elementary stood on the makeshift stage in their angel costumes and sang "Santa Claus Is Coming to Town" accompanied by the quartet who'd volunteered to provide the musical entertainment for the evening. Faith knew she could finally breathe and enjoy herself a little.

Her pleasure stood just a few feet away, leaning against a barn post with his hands in the pockets of a pair of black slacks. The white button-down shirt he wore with the long sleeves rolled up to his elbows, and his dark hair neatly combed back, added a bit of old-world elegance. For whatever reason, he'd forgone the boots and hat for the evening. Too bad. She kind of liked him looking tough and rugged. She wouldn't even mind seeing him a little messed up, minus the boots, pants, and shirt.

But she digressed.

Apparently a lot where he was concerned.

Temptation overruled sanity, and as she walked up to him, the heat in his eyes reached out and enfolded her in a secret, sexy embrace. Her nipples responded. So did parts further south. She wondered if his thoughts might be headed in the same direction. The sudden smile that lifted his masculine lips said yes.

Every day for the past two weeks, he'd been right there by her side, helping with whatever needed to be done and never complaining. Even though the tragedy of his father's death still haunted him. Even though he was a paying guest who should have been relaxing and enjoying all the activities and luxuries the ranch offered. He worked. All day. At night, when he could have gone into town to kick up his heels, he'd stayed with her to shuck away the day's undertakings.

Sometimes they enjoyed a glass of wine by the fire. Sometimes a bowl of ice cream or a slice of Shelby's fabulous cinnamon apple pie. Afterward, they'd share a healthy dose of passion that included kissing and caresses that could have easily led to the bedroom. Or the leather sofa. Or the floor. But Chase had held back. At the end of the night, he'd go back to his own cabin, leaving her to climb the stairs to her bedroom.

Alone.

With too much time to think and wonder why.

"Congratulations," he drawled with the tiniest hint of his Texas roots. "Looks like the party is a success."

"It's exceeding my expectations." She smiled as he slowly reached out and tucked a strand of her hair behind her ear. "I just checked the silent-auction bids, and they're through the roof. The only one that's lacking is old Chester Banks's horseback-riding-lesson package deal. You know, the one that says *Ladies Only*."

Chase laughed. "For an old guy, he is a pretty big flirt."

"Which is why the ladies are probably shying away."

"Maybe I should go place a bid."

"But you already know how to ride."

"He doesn't know that. Besides, it's for charity."

"I think you're the wrong kind of student he's got in mind. You'd look horrible in a skirt."

"Like I said." He shrugged. "It's for charity. I'm sure not even the flirtatious old geezer could argue with that."

"Well, Chester may not appreciate it, but my organization would be most appreciative." She leaned in and kissed his smooth-shaven cheek. While her hormones sighed, she managed a simple, "Thank you."

"Just how appreciative would that be?"

The naughty sparkle in his eyes set off all kinds of luscious, naked, sweaty thoughts in her head. She laughed. "Are you trying to buy me off?"

He reached down and took her hand. "Would you let me?"

Laughter bubbled up in her chest. "It depends."

His head tilted. "On?"

She leaned in, and his delicious scent danced like a magic elixir through her quickly heating blood. "On how much you're willing to pay."

"I'm all in." His eyes met hers as his thumb caressed the sensitive skin over the top of her hand. "The rest is your call."

Exhilaration and anticipation danced through her blood. No sense being coy, she wanted him. Heck, she'd wanted him weeks ago. As she glanced around at her friends and family, who were having a great time, she couldn't help thinking that another entire hour to wait for Chase to hold her in his arms seemed like an eternity. But her responsibilities weren't over. She couldn't just walk out and leave her guests. So she said, "After the party's over, I'll meet you in front of the Christmas tree in the lodge."

As she turned back to her remaining duties, she stopped, and went back to him. "Come prepared to play with some high stakes." She let her eyes glide down and back up his body. "And I'm not talking cold hard cash."

His jaw dropped. Just enough to let her know she'd caught him by surprise. But his follow-up grin said he was indeed all in.

Chapter Seven

LATE INTO THE EVENING, the air had turned cool. Cold enough, actually, to send shivers down Faith's arms as she waved good-bye to the last guest, then walked from the barn to the lodge house. When she lit the fire in the hearth, the heat from the whoosh of flames felt good against her palms as she held them out in front of her.

Just as she'd hoped, the event tonight had gone smooth. Her organization had profited well, which meant she'd have more funds to buy Christmas gifts for the kids and to open the doors to the ranch for several more children. Last summer, she'd had an idea to turn custom-built covered wagons and teepees into sleeping quarters for her young campers. The extra cash the silent and live auctions had brought in would go toward making that concept a reality.

She had Chase to thank for all the efforts he'd put in behind the scenes. Even so, he'd refused to let her publicly acknowledge his help. So many questions about him filtered through her mind. What were his plans? Where would he go and what would he do after he left the ranch? While it had been a more than pleasant surprise when he'd extended his stay again, according to the reservation books, he'd be leaving soon.

But would he?

Would he decide to stay even longer? Or with Christmas only a few days away, would he choose to go home to his family for the holidays? Or would he run to try to avoid the memories?

With all that said and done, where would that leave her?

He owed her nothing.

The trouble came because, when she hadn't been looking, he'd filled the emptiness in her life and her heart she hadn't even known existed. She'd always consumed herself with the ranch, been too busy, thought she'd been too damaged from her past relationship to ever feel this way again. But Chase had effortlessly worked his way into her life, her routine, her thoughts, and her dreams.

With any luck, tonight he'd work his way into her bed.

He made her feel alive again. Made her visualize a future she hadn't dared to believe could ever happen. Unfortunately, all of those were one-sided thoughts.

The question remained, what did he think of her?

She glanced up at the mantel clock, where the red-and-amber glow from the flames in the hearth reflected off the glass. The party had been over for a while, and the guests had long gone home. She'd left the mess in the barn to be cleaned up the following day and had gone in the house to freshen up. And wait.

Would he even show?

WHEN FAITH HAD left the barn, waved to the last departing guest and gone into the lodge, Chase stayed behind to clean things up a bit. The task could have waited till morning, but he hoped that tomorrow when the sun rose he'd be too busy holding Faith in his arms and making love to her. He'd gone back to his cabin for a quick shower, and, for the first time since the day he'd arrived, he smiled at the fencepost snowman that stood guard at his door.

Now his feet couldn't move fast enough through the chill of the night air and down the lit pathway. Above him, the icicle lights twinkled in the wide-spreading oak branches. In front of him . . . what? His destiny?

Anxious, he didn't bother to knock and, instead, swung the front door wide open. Traditional Christmas music greeted him along with a tail-wagging Doc, who waited for a little rub between his ears before trotting off.

When Chase stepped around the dividing wall and into the great room, he found Faith standing before the fire in a different dress than the one she'd worn to the barn dance. This one fell to her bare ankles in soft, clingy waves of silky white fabric.

The dancing firelight outlined her luscious curves, which often tended to be hidden beneath a baggy work shirt. Beside her, the twinkling lights on the tree created a magic he had never captured in any of the advertising projects he'd worked on over the years.

She must have showered because she'd put her hair up, and some of the thick honey curls that escaped capture, were damp and dangling over her smooth shoulders.

"Damn."

At his exclamation, she turned. Smiled. Then held out her hand and offered him a . . . toasted marshmallow?

"Don't need that," he said. "You look good enough to eat."

He strode over to her, and, instead of accepting the marshmallow she held out, he wrapped his palm at the back of her nape, then slid the fingers of both hands into her hair and covered her mouth with his.

With both her hands occupied, she couldn't wrap them around him, but he didn't mind. Her sweet mouth was doing all the talking he needed at that moment. At her inhaled surprise, he jumped at the opportunity of her parted lips, stroking his tongue against hers, making love to her mouth until she leaned in and plastered herself to his chest.

Missing her touch, he took a momentary break, lifted his head, and eyed the toasted puffs between her fingers. "Why are you holding marshmallows?"

Her eyes blinked open, dazed, then she smiled. "Celebration S'mores shooters."

Peering inside, he realized the marshmallow had been scooped out, and the toasted shell had become a shot glass for a splash of rich coffee liqueur.

"Clever." He accepted his, and they toasted, consuming the marshmallow cup as well. When they were done, Faith licked her fingers while smiling up at him. His momentary break shattered, and he pulled her back into his arms. He teased his tongue across her lips, savoring the sweet marshmallow like she was a Christmas treat.

"I want your hands on me," he said, looking own into her upturned face. "All over me. And then I want to pour the rest of that liqueur all over you and lick it off. Slowly."

Her flirty smile turned seductress. "Good thing I just bought a new bottle."

"We have all night. Right?"

"All." She dragged her fingertip from his top lip down to the bottom. "Night." She leaned in and snagged his lower lip gently between her teeth. "Long."

"Then I suggest we don't waste any more time." He lowered his head and kissed her, delving deep into her mouth and enjoying the sweet taste of the liqueur on her tongue. Her arms curled around his neck, and the firmness of her breasts pressed deliciously into his chest. He slipped his hands down to her full, sexy hips, then slowly, inch by inch, drew her silky dress up into his hands until most of it was bunched in his palms.

Then he eased the fabric up.

When the silk came off, Chase was thrilled to find that beneath that seductive dress, Faith had only bothered to slip on the tiniest pair of white lace panties with a little white bow at the top.

Firelight and the glittering of the tree lights highlighted her gorgeous, shapely body like a Peter Paul

Rubens masterpiece as she stood back and let him look. Never in his life had he been more grateful for a woman who allowed herself to enjoy a bowl of ice cream after a hard day at work, then had the confidence to stand before him and not to try to hide all her luscious curves and dimples.

His heart rate kicked into a zone he'd never reached before, but he had no fears that it would cause him any pain.

Just the opposite.

He reached out, removed the clip from her hair, and watched as the soft curls tumbled over her bare shoulders and down her back.

"My God, you're gorgeous." Passion ignited the thick arousal surging through his veins.

"You might be gorgeous too." Her head tilted, and a smile brushed her lips. "Hard to tell with all those clothes on."

Laughter tickled his chest, and he surrendered to the heated curiosity in her eyes. He held his arms. "Maybe you can remedy that problem."

She came forward, and he was immediately consumed with her honeyed scent. He wanted his hands all over her—now—and he didn't think she'd argue if he took her hard and fast. But with her, he wasn't in for a lightning round. Tonight, he wanted a pleasure cruise.

"I hope you came prepared to play." She smiled up at him while her fingers trailed down the front of his shirt, unbuttoning it along the way. When the cotton fabric hung free from his shoulders, her warm fingers played over his chest, ran through the short hairs, then tweaked his hard nipples.

Her soft, seductive laughter rippled through him like the slow build to a hot orgasm. Then she leaned in, kissed his chest, and slicked her tongue across his nipple. "Mmmm. Definitely gorgeous."

Unable to bear the heavy lust pounding through his veins another second, he kicked off his shoes, yanked a rag quilt off the back of the sofa along with a couple of pillows, and tossed them on the rug in front of the fireplace. Then he pulled her up into his arms until her legs wrapped around his waist. Her sweet scent engulfed him, made him even hungrier for her.

As the fire crackled in the hearth, and Michael Bublé crooned, "Baby, please come home for Christmas," Chase eased her down to the floor.

"Playtime's over, sweet thing. Time to get down to business."

FAITH HAD KNOWN lust before. She'd known love. But she'd never had the two collide in such a spectacular way as when Chase laid her on the floor and rose above her with such a heady look of desire in his green eyes. It made her head spin.

They'd spent nearly every evening together for the past couple of weeks, and they'd gotten to know each other well. She knew he was a man she could trust with her heart.

But right now, she planned give him her body.

It seemed a great place to start.

He slid his palms down the small of her back and lifted her so he could hold her close to his chest. Kiss her mouth. And make everything inside her cry out for more. Between them, his erection pressed hot and hard against the thin lace of her panties.

"I want you so bad, I can barely hold back," he murmured against her mouth. "I feel like a teenager in the backseat of my daddy's old Chevy."

"No need to hold back." She moaned as his mouth moved hot and moist down the side of her neck. "I want you bad too."

He tipped his head back just enough to look in her eyes. "That's not the way this is going to work, Faith. We're going to take all night doing this. I know your mind. Now I want to know your body."

Who could argue with a sentiment like that? Especially when his tongue was trailing across her shoulder, and he was cupping her breasts in his hands and lowering his head to drag a slow, wet lick across her sensitive, peaked nipple. In the fervor of soft touches and hungry strokes, he slipped his hands down her waist, hooked his thumbs in her panties, and pulled them off. When he leaned back to discard them, she realized he still had way too many clothes on.

"I'm game. But if we're going to make this a marathon, I'd like to be able to touch you too." She glided her hands over his smooth, muscled chest, then curled her fingers in his shirt and tugged it off his shoulders. When his upper body was bare to her touch, a sigh escaped her lips. Her greedy palms caressed the expanse of that strong chest where the short, soft hair spread between his flat brown nipples, then dipped to a thin trail that swirled his belly button and disappeared behind his zipper.

"Mmmm. Much better." She reached for his waistband. "Pants too."

He moved away, just enough to give her access to his zipper. He quickly removed the slacks along with a pair of black boxer briefs. And then he was back, settled between her legs, erection pressed hotly against her pelvis. He slid his hands up her thighs, over her belly, and cupped her breasts for better access as he took one swollen bud into his mouth, glided his tongue along the crest, and gave a gentle pull with his lips.

Desire burned through her veins as he kissed his way down her stomach and parted her slick folds with his thumbs. Then he looked up at her from between her legs, a seductive glimmer sparked in his eyes.

"I want *all* of you, Faith."

Anticipation locked down everything inside her except the awareness of him. She couldn't move, couldn't even nod as he lowered his head between her legs and teased her tingling core with the flat of his warm tongue. She dropped her head back and closed her eyes. Sensation took charge, and with a moan that swelled on each slide of his tongue, she knew at that moment she would give him anything he asked for.

WHEN FAITH CAME apart beneath his hands and the pressure of his tongue, Chase ignored the needy pulsations in his cock and savored the moment.

Head back, eyes closed, her hands were on her large, firm breasts, fingers plucking her nipples. Her thigh muscles tensed and pressed into his shoulders while her orgasm tasted like honey on his lips. With firelight dancing in her hair and playing across her soft skin, he knew he'd never seen anything more beautiful. Hunger rolled over him in an uncontainable wave, and the moment her heavy panting began to subside into fulfilled moans, he slid up her warm body. She welcomed him into her arms, wrapped her legs around his hips, and drew him down.

He meant to take his time.

To make slow, sweet love to her.

But when the head of his cock nudged the entrance of her hot, moist, tight body, he realized that might have to be on the second round. When she reached between them and gave him a long, firm stroke, he dove into the pleasure of her touch.

Anxious to feel her surrounding him, he grabbed a condom from his pants pocket, tore open the packet, and she took the pleasure of rolling on the latex.

With a long sigh, she guided him in. As he fully pushed into her, her body stretched to accept all of him, and her sweet warmth surrounded him. Urgency pumped through his veins, his lungs clutched, and his gut constricted. Embedded deep, he somehow managed to maintain control–even as his dick urged him to push harder and faster. And though he loved hearing her moan his name, the breathy little noises she made weren't helping his control.

"Oh, God. Chase." She let go a sexy sigh. "You feel so good. Harder, baby. Please."

He pushed in deeper simply because he had no choice. His body had overruled all his good intentions. He retreated and advanced again, giving in to the absolute pleasure and sensation of being inside her luscious body.

Over and over he thrust. Slow. Steady. Gentle. Fast. Hard. Deep. All the while, he watched the expressions of passion on her beautiful face. She made him want to last forever just to keep that smile on her lips.

Then her thick lashes fluttered open. When their eyes met, she wrapped her fingers around his nape and drew his head down for a kiss.

"Now, Chase." Her hips arched up to meet his thrust. "I'm about to explode. Give me everything you've got. Right . . ." She met his thrust again. Her inner muscles clenched around him. Pulled him in tighter. "Now."

The tension and ache in his cock burst like a dam in an explosion of hot, heavy sensation. The vibration of her orgasm radiated along his shaft and squeezed. Pleasure swept across his skin, and he let go with a deep groan that came from somewhere deep in his soul. When she curled her arms around him and sighed with contentment against his chest, he knew he'd found something he'd never expected the day he arrived at the Magic Box Guest Ranch.

Or maybe ever.

Chapter Eight

"I DON'T KNOW what to do with you now."

Chase lifted his head from the soft pillow, leaned on an elbow, and noted Faith's very contented smile. They'd made love again after they'd come upstairs to her bed, and now they lay tangled up in each other. It was the most blissful state he'd ever experienced except when he was inside her warm body.

"You ready to get rid of me already?" he asked.

"No." She chuckled. "But you're a paying guest, and we just did *that*. Several times. So now I don't know whether to not charge you for your cabin or–"

"How about I stay right here with you?" He kissed the tip of her nose. "In your bed."

Her gray eyes widened just slightly. "For the rest of your stay?"

He nodded.

"But won't that seem like I'm charging you for . . . sex?

Like a hot-stone massage or something?" She pressed a hand to her forehead. "I wouldn't even know how much to charge. I mean, I've never done that–"

He silenced her with his mouth, tasting the sweetness of her kiss, knowing he wanted to close his eyes at night with the taste of her on his tongue and wake each morning with it on his lips.

He chuckled. "You're ridiculous."

"I know. But I've never been in this position before."

"Are you worried about what the others will think?"

"Of course not." Her fingertips caressed his cheek. "You should know by now I play by my own set of rules. They just wouldn't want to see me get hurt."

"Neither would I," he said. And meant it. "Ask me to stay, Faith."

After a long pause she said, "I can't, Chase. You have a lot of healing and exploring to do to find your place in the world again. But for tonight, I'm all yours."

When he began to protest, she pressed her finger to his lips. "One day at a time," she said. "Then if it ends, neither of us will be hurt."

He didn't concur.

He didn't oppose.

But later that night, after a dinner of cowboy grilled steak and the ice-cream-sundae desserts they'd prepared together, he moved into the lodge house and into her bed.

TWO DAYS AFTER the charity barn dance and two luxurious nights spent in the haven of Faith's arms, Chase found himself pushing a wobbly cart through the store, following her lead through the toy department.

"Why are girls so consumed with Barbie?" he wanted to know.

She looked up from the pink boxes in her hands and laughed. "Beats me. I've never been able to figure that out. Maybe it comes from our insatiable craving for perfection. Even when we're just children."

He leaned in and stole a kiss. "I think you're perfect."

A little sigh pushed through her lips as she dropped the boxes down into the ever-growing pile of toys in the cart. "Chase Morgan, are you going to make me so hot and needy I have to drag you into the furniture department and have my way with you?"

"Yes." He smiled.

She laughed. "Okay, just let me finish with the items on this list first. Kids before lust."

He kissed her again and refrained from sharing his thoughts that sometimes kids came from lust. And that was okay with him too. A surprising revelation since he'd never really considered having his own family before.

Faith had changed everything.

The easiness and familiarity between them had been like this from the moment they'd gone skin on skin. Heart-to-heart. Somehow it seemed like they'd gone beyond the physical and made some kind of metaphysical connection that night. He couldn't figure it out, and he wasn't complaining. Except for the fact that she currently had him working as her personal assistant in a superstore with big rollback signs and people running around in blue vests.

He'd never been in a Walmart before. Hell, in New York, the only shopping he'd ever done in an actual brick-and-mortar store had been to stop in at the neighborhood grocer when he ran out of something. His shopping had been either done online or by his administrative assistant. His groceries had been brought in by the woman he'd hired to maintain his house. And most nights he ate dinner out.

Faith checked off everything on her pink aisle list, and they rounded the end cap into what Chase would have to describe as Transformers Alley. He almost laughed. Once upon a time, he'd given his best shot to secure the advertising contract for the summer blockbuster movie. He could have made millions. Now he was just as happy watching the woman in front of him picking through boxes of the much-desired toys like they were candy. Each action figure she selected would go to an under-privileged child. And that was better any day of the week than picking up a hefty paycheck.

Focused on the fit of Faith's delectable derriere in her Wranglers, Chase flinched as a woman in a vibrant blue muumuu and orthopedic shoes grabbed his arm.

Bright red smeared her crinkled lips as her mouth dropped open, and she gasped. "Fancy seeing you here. I thought you'd be headed back to New York by now."

"Hello, Mrs. Lewis. Don't you look pretty today."

"Oh." The elderly woman blushed and fanned herself, kicking up an overpowering scent of menthol that made his eyes tear. "*You* can call me Gladys."

Faith came back down the aisle and dropped four Optimus Prime Transformer action figures into the cart. "I talked him into helping me with shopping for the charity Christmas morning," she said. "Then, most likely, he'll head back."

"Trying to get rid of me again?" Chase didn't like the sudden detachment in her voice.

She shrugged. "Just accepting reality."

Gladys's rheumy eyes darted between the two of them. "Well, that's too bad. Be nice for you to have a man around the ranch."

"Don't forget Bull," Faith said. "He's quite a lot of help with everything. So what are you buying today, Mrs. Lewis?"

Faith's detour in conversation raised the hairs on the back of Chase's neck. Like someone had flipped a switch, she went from hot to cold.

And he didn't like it.

"Epsom salts. The weather's suddenly going colder kicked in the gout in my danged feet. Before they go purple on me, they need a long soak. Then I'll be good as new and ready to boogie."

After delivering that bit of wretched information, Gladys gave them a wave and walked away, orthopedic shoes squeaking on the tile floor.

Chase turned to Faith. "What was that all about?"

She pulled a Paw Patrol On-A-Roll Marshall and Fire Truck from the shelf and tossed it in the cart. Then she dragged her attention away from the list in her hand and met his gaze.

"I love being with you, Chase. But I'm not crazy

enough to try to convince myself that you're going to stay here forever. You worked hard for your career and your life in New York. You'd be a fool to just walk away. Despite what happened to you, you're smart enough to figure out how to blend the passion you have for your work and your new outlook on life. And . . ." Her shoulders lifted on a sigh. "As much as I want you to be here, I know I'd never be enough."

Her ex-fiancé's slur hung silently between them.

All you really are is a hillbilly who should never have left the farm.

Stunned, Chase watched her walk away. This time her honesty hit him like a sucker punch.

But this time she was wrong.

Faith was the most incredible woman he'd ever met in his life. And he'd met plenty. As smart as she was, he couldn't believe she'd buy into the bullshit that jerk had tried to feed her. But as he knew, sometimes wounds went deep, and it appeared Faith had become the victim of some old-fashioned bullying.

For years, Chase had viewed Christmas as the enemy. The one constant in his life that wounded him over and over again. Faith had opened his eyes and his heart. And for the first time in what felt like forever, he looked forward to the celebration. But mostly he looked forward to opening his eyes on Christmas day and seeing her beautiful face first thing.

The past was past.

And at the moment, the future looked damned bright.

Chapter Nine

EARLY CHRISTMAS MORNING, Chase woke with Faith warm and sweet in his arms and Doc settled in at the bottom of the bed around their feet. The night before after they'd wrapped what seemed like umpteen hundred gifts, they'd made love with insatiable hunger.

On her part, it seemed like she thought it was their last time together. On his side, the hunger came because the more time they spent together, the more he wanted her.

How had they become so unbalanced when just a few days ago it seemed as though they were both on the same page?

Beside him, he felt her come awake and enjoyed the little sigh she hummed as she nestled her luscious body closer.

She turned her head and smiled up at him. "Merry Christmas."

"Merry Christmas." He kissed the tip of her nose.

"This is the best I've had since I was eight years old and got my very own horse."

She chuckled. "You're comparing me to a horse?"

He shook his head. "Comparing you to the best gift I ever received."

"Awww." She turned to face him, pressing her plump breasts against his chest and wrapping her leg around his thigh. "You say the nicest things."

"I do?"

She nodded, and the silk of her hair glided across his chest. "And memorable too. I believe one of the first things you ever said to me was that you'd eat anything."

He laughed and hugged her close. Then he proceeded to prove there were more delicious things to devour than a morning breakfast of eggs and toast.

AFTER HER SHOWER, Faith came down the stairs literally glowing from the passion she just shared with Chase. No need for makeup today. When she'd looked in the mirror the woman looking back had a radiance that could only be caused by two things. Making love. And being in love.

Check.

And check.

Since she'd escaped Houston, she'd never spent a Christmas alone. And with the exuberant group that would arrive shortly, she wouldn't spend this one alone either. Besides the children and their parents, who'd arrive to accept the gifts given by her charity, Paige and

Aiden would be there as well as Bull and Shelby and her boys. Even if they didn't all show, she'd have Chase.

But for how long?

How long before he got tired of playing house with her and flew back to Manhattan and picked up where he'd left off with his exciting, fast-paced life? How long before he realized he'd left slow-moving Texas a long time ago for a reason?

When she got halfway down the stairs, the scent of warm cinnamon buns tickled her nose. The lights were already aglow on the enormous tree, whose lower branches now rested on the cheerfully wrapped presents waiting to be enjoyed by all. A blaze crackled in the hearth. And Bing Crosby serenaded her with "White Christmas."

Faith's heart expanded and sighed.

Someone had been busy while she showered.

"Come here, sweet thing." Chase's deep voice called out from the foyer. Curious, she went to find him, wondering what he might need help with before their company arrived. When she cleared the dividing wall, she found him at the front door, smiling.

"Are the guests arriving already?" She laughed. "The eager beavers."

"No." He shook his head. "But I ordered a gift for you, and it finally arrived."

"For me?" Her hand settled against her chest. Beneath her fingertips, her heart pounded. "You didn't have to."

He held out his hand, drew her to his side, and looked down into her face. "This was my father's favorite song. You gave me back the ability to listen to it for the first time since he died. You're an incredible, special woman, Faith. And as much as I'd like to claim ownership of what I'm about to show you, I think the gift came from someone much higher up than I."

Before she had a chance to respond to the warmth of his words, he lowered his head and kissed her so sweetly, it brought tears to her eyes.

"You said you'd never had a white Christmas . . ." Chase opened the double doors.

Faith gasped.

"Now you have."

Everything was covered in white. The ground. The corral posts. The roof of the barn. Doc's furry back as he frolicked and rolled around, snuffling his nose beneath layers and layers of white. Fat, fluffy snowflakes fell from the sky in a perfect shower of glistening snow.

"Oh my . . ." She grabbed Chase's hand and rushed outside, pulling him behind her. When they cleared the cover of the veranda, she let go, lifted her palms to the sky, and spun in a circle. She stuck out her tongue and felt the icy flakes melt.

"Snow angels!" She grabbed Chase's hand again and pulled him to the ground. Beside her, he chuckled. Then they both spread their arms and legs to make angels in the thick fluff of snow.

Though the cold seeped through the back of her clothes, she lay on the ground looking up into the gray sky, and smiled. "Best Christmas ever."

When Chase leaned over her and pulled her into his arms, her heart gave a happy sigh.

"Merry Christmas, sweet thing," Chase murmured. Then he lowered his head and pressed a kiss to her lips that absolutely sealed her belief that magic came in all kinds of shapes and sizes.

WITHIN A FEW HOURS, not an ounce of room remained in the grand living space of the lodge house at the Magic Box Guest Ranch. While the children sat on the floor beside the twinkling tree and the glowing hearth, chattering like mice about their new gifts, their parents sat about enjoying the atmosphere and the sweet hot chocolate Chase had prepared with Faith earlier after they'd brushed off the snow and gone back inside.

Along with the group that benefited from the generosity of Faith's charity work, were her sister Paige, Aiden, Shelby, and her three boys, and Bull, who'd played the role of Santa Claus so perfectly that Chase had almost been fooled into believing the jolly old elf actually existed. He'd never seen the old man smile until today. Since then, Bull hadn't been able to turn off the grin that beamed from behind the fake beard.

Across the room, Faith sat on the floor beside a little girl named Megan he'd been introduced to earlier. The child had disabilities that made it difficult for her to push the buttons on the play cell phone the charity had purchased for her. With a smile, Faith pulled a miniature magic wand from her pocket and handed it to Megan. The wand had a stylus on the end and allowed the child to successfully enjoy her new toy.

If he hadn't already, Chase would have fallen in love right then and there.

The doorbell rang, and Chase looked up.

Faith smiled, giving him an, *I'm kinda busy here could you get the door?* shrug.

Happy to comply, Chase acknowledged the absolute joy filling the space around him as he opened the door.

"Surprise!"

"Merry Christmas, big brother!"

If he'd not felt the spirit of giving before, Chase was overwhelmed by its presence as Boone and Cassidy wrapped him in a family hug. He wondered if they'd call him a total sap if he cried. Probably. And he didn't care.

"Merry Christmas." Beside him, Faith looked up with a smile so warm he felt it all the way into his heart.

Overwhelmed with emotion, he couldn't speak. So he curled his arm around her and drew her into their circle.

When they finally all stepped back, Chase provided the introductions. Although Faith had provided the surprise, she'd only spoken to his siblings by phone. Moments later, as Boone and Cassidy headed into the great room to join the others, Chase caught Faith's hand and drew her into his arms.

"Thank you."

"You're welcome." She smiled, lifted to her toes, and pressed a kiss to his mouth. "I called your mother too, but she wasn't able to come."

"Doesn't matter." He tightened his embrace. "I've got everything I need right here."

AFTER THE PRESENTS had been opened and the gift wrappings discarded, the group of family and friends shared more hot chocolate, steaming coffee, and thick slices of the sweet pumpkin pie Shelby had provided for the celebration.

Later, while the snow still fell from the gray sky, Chase closed the door behind the last remaining guests. Boone and Cassidy were in their own cabins on the ranch, and Chase finally had Faith all to himself.

He found her on the sofa, head back, eyes closed. As he passed by, he bent over and gave her an upside-down kiss.

"Time to relax." She patted the sofa, while Doc settled down on the rug in front of the fire in the roaring hearth. "Come sit beside me."

He settled in next to her, but before he could tuck her into his arms, she reached beneath a pillow, pulled out a small, gift-wrapped box, and handed it to him.

"Merry Christmas," she said. "I know you'll probably be leaving soon. And this isn't much but . . . well, open it, and I'll explain."

She'd given him the gift of bringing his family together for the holiday, so he hadn't expected anything more. But the sweetness of the gesture warmed his heart, which was already overflowing.

Never able to contain himself with unwrapping gifts, he tore off the shiny red bow and gold paper, then removed the lid of the black box. Inside lay a gold instrument on a bed of white satin. When he looked up, Faith's gray eyes glittered.

"It's a compass," she said.

"I can see that."

"So you can always find your way back."

"To you?"

She nodded, and a single tear caught like a diamond on her bottom lashes.

"I do have to go back to New York," he said. "I have business there."

Again, she nodded. "I know."

"No, sweet thing . . ." Before she could look away he caught her chin between his fingers. "I don't think you do. So I want you to listen carefully. Okay?"

"Okay."

"I have to go back to New York . . . to tie things up. Close things out. Put my apartment up for sale and get the rest of the stink of the city off me." He smiled at the reference she'd thrown out the very first day they'd met.

"You what?" Her eyes glittered again. This time with curiosity.

"Ask me to come back, Faith." He kissed her tasty lips. "Ask me to stay. Not because you need another hand around the ranch. Not because you need someone to push your shopping cart when you fill it full of presents. Ask me because you want me here because you think you might be falling in love with me."

She blinked, and the tears were back. "I don't have to think," she said. "I *know* I'm falling in love with you."

Warmth filled his soul. "That first night when you fell into my arms—"

"Literally." She laughed.

"Perfectly," he said. "I already knew."

"You knew what?"

"That day we went shopping for the gifts? You said you knew you'd never be enough to keep me here. Faith, you're not only enough, you're more than I ever expected." He kissed her trembling bottom lip. "More than I ever dreamed. Thank you for this gift. It's very special, but I don't really need it. I know where I belong."

"I–"

"Ssssh." He smiled, pressed a finger to her lips. "My turn." He reached beneath the sofa and rolled out the long cardboard tube he'd covered with a cheerful dancing-snowmen gift wrap. "This is for you."

"But . . ." She took the present and held it against her chest. "You didn't have to get me anything."

"Open the gift, Faith."

She sniffed. "Okay."

Carefully, her fingers untied the ribbon, then pulled off the paper and the end of the tube. She reached inside and withdrew the rolled papers.

"The first one is a marketing plan along with a financial schedule that will allow you to double the number of children who can visit each summer," he explained while she unrolled the paper in her hands. When she smiled up at him, he eagerly helped her unroll the second paper. "And this is a blueprint for the covered-wagon sleeping quarters you want to build."

"Where did you get these?"

"I called in a favor from a friend. Do you like them?"

"Like?" She shook her head. "Love? Yes."

"I'm glad."

"Thank you." She curled her arm around his neck and kissed his cheek. "This is so thoughtful. And it will be the gift that keeps on giving."

"There's more."

"More?" She wrinkled her nose. "Chase, this is more than enough. It's wonderful."

"I didn't give you those plans because I expect you to accomplish them all on your own. I'm selfish. I want to be a part of it. I want to be a part of your life, Faith. A part of the Magic Box Ranch. Forever. If you'll have me."

"Pretty words from an adman."

"Pretty words with meaning." He pulled the small white box from between the sofa cushions and handed it to her. "Say yes, Faith. Ask me to stay. Tell me you want me to be in your life forever. Give me the best Christmas I'll ever know."

She opened the box and revealed the solitaire diamond he'd taken a chance and bought because he already knew he couldn't live without her.

Her fingers fluttered to her mouth, then she looked up at him and sighed a "Yes."

His heart leaped.

"On one condition," she said.

"Which is?"

"That each Christmas will only get better and better."

"Then let this be the first of many." He drew her into his arms and, heart-thumping happily, he kissed her soft and slow.

For a man who'd once seen Christmas as a painful reminder of his loss, he acknowledged the error of his ways and accepted the most precious gift he'd ever received.

"Merry Christmas, Faith. I love you." He gently stroked her cheeks, catching her happy tears with his fingertips. "With all my heart."

And for a man whose heart just weeks ago had completely stopped . . . that was really saying something.

**Can't get enough of
Candis Terry's Sweet, Texas?
This winter, get ready for a**

Sweet Surprise

Fiona Wilder knows all about falling in lust. Love? That's another story. Determined not to repeat past mistakes, the single mom and cupcake-shop owner is focused on walking the straight and narrow. But trouble has a way of finding her. And this time it comes in the form of a smoking-hot firefighter who knows all the delicious ways to ignite her bad-girl fuse.

Firefighter Mike Halsey learned long ago that playing with fire just gets you burned. He's put his demons behind him, and if there's one line he won't cross, it's getting involved with his best friend's ex. But when fate throws him in the path of the beautiful, strong, and off-limits Fiona, will he be able to fight their attraction? Or will he willingly go down in flames?

**Coming February 2015
from Avon Books
Keep reading for a sneak peek . . .**

FIONA WILDER DID not like being the center of attention. The intense scrutiny never failed to make her feel like she had toilet paper stuck to the bottom of her shoe, or that the back of her dress was caught up in her panty hose and her rearview assets were out there for everyone to observe.

And judge.

At the moment, however, while she might be near the focal point of every hungry pair of female eyes in the vicinity, she wasn't necessarily the nucleus. That honor went to the man she happened to be dancing with at the wedding reception of Reno and Charlotte Wilder.

As just one of their numerous preceremony calamities, Reno and Charli's postnuptial festivities had needed to be relocated from a flooded reception hall to Jesse Wilder's backyard oasis. The picturesque landscape had been transformed into a wedding wonderland of twinkling fairy lights, floating lotus candles in a natural, stone-edged pool, and elegant tables set with fabulous centerpieces of curly willow branches and fragrant roses.

Not a surprise that Fiona found the romantic atmosphere far superior to anything a dusty old reception hall could offer. On the other hand, she couldn't be more surprised to find herself in the arms of Mr. Tall, Dark, and Delicious.

AKA firefighter Mike Halsey.

Previously, he'd been one of the bachelors up for auction at the Black Ties and Levi's charity event to raise funds for the expansion of the Sweet Emergency Center. On that particular night, she'd either been too chicken or not nearly schnockered enough to raise her paddle and bid on him even though just the sight of his extreme hotness in those fitted Levi's, crisp white shirt, and black tux jacket practically had her bid paddle melting in her lap. In the end, her former mother-in-law, Jana, had plunked down a good amount of cash to *win* Mike. Though what the woman planned to do with him remained to be seen.

The truth behind the reason Fiona's paddle had stayed put also came as no surprise.

At least not to her.

Since the dissolution of her and Jackson Wilder's short but meaningful marriage, she'd pushed aside any type of personal involvement with the opposite sex. Not that she'd decided to play for the other team or anything, she'd just been too busy repenting for her failures and playing the role of single mom to their four-year-old, Isabella.

Plus there was the minor little detail of the whole trust issue thing she had going on with herself. Instead of graduating, as she had, with a business degree from Clemson, you would have thought she'd acquired a master's degree in *How to Screw Up Your Life*.

There had never been any doubt that Jackson was an amazing dad to Izzy, and Fiona considered him one of the best men she'd ever known. He just hadn't been the best man for her. Likewise, she hadn't been the right woman for him. Fortunately, they loved and respected each other and totally rocked as best friends and unified parents.

Life sure had a funny way of working things out.

Since their divorce, Jackson had rediscovered Abby, the true love of his life. Abby also happened to be his very first love, which he foolishly let go. Now Jackson and Abby were next in line to walk down the aisle, and Fiona truly couldn't be more delighted for them. To know the universe had somehow righted itself sent bubbles of happiness through her heart.

To that end, and because someday she'd like to find that same kind of relationship bliss for herself, she'd done everything in her power to banish *Naughty Fiona*—her inner wild child–an insatiable party girl who had a tendency to fall in lust, not love, with gorgeous firemen or men of that same dashing-daredevil breed. The kind of men who possessed sculpted calendar-boy faces, perfect pecs, rippled abs, and tight buns. The kind of men who appeared to be unattainable and whom she now considered off-limits.

She didn't have time anyway. Her plate was full with building a happy and prosperous future for her and Izzy. She might have messed up a lot earlier in her life by being foolish and reckless, but she wouldn't let that happen again.

Naughty Fiona was on lockdown in bad-girl solitary confinement.

As the reception band's lively cover of "Beer Money" came to an end, and the two-steppin' couples cleared the floor, Fiona gave sexy Fireman Mike a smile of thanks for the dance. He returned the gesture with a megawatt grin. But as the band rolled into Keith Urban's sexy tune "Raining on Sunday," Mike maintained a gentle grip on her hand.

She looked up into his dark-as-sin eyes, and a warm tingle traveled from her traitorous fingers down into areas that had been restrained so long they teetered on the point of a jailbreak.

"How about another dance?" Mike's smile amped up to blinding. "We didn't get a chance to talk much on that last one."

Nervous energy rippled through her body. She knew that the envious scowls coming from the females in the crowd who were waiting eagerly for *their* chance at Mr. Hottie McFireman would soon turn to daggers. And since her naughty side had lusted after the man since that night at the bachelor auction, all the more reason to politely decline.

But then, that big firefighting, lifesaving hand reeled

her back into his embrace—close enough to catch the manly scent of warm skin, citrusy aftershave, and palpable sexuality.

Heaven help her, it was like waving a red flag at a charging bull.

"I'd love to."

Yeah. No way in all the Land of Oz would her naughty self give up a chance like this.

Sorry ladies-in-waiting, let the dagger glares commence.

And let the trouble begin.

AFTER MONTHS OF being unable to get his best friend's ex-wife off his mind, Mike finally had his hands on her. Regrettably for him, a simple dance was about as far as he could ever allow himself to go.

Not that he didn't want to dip his nose into the soft slope of Fiona's delicate neck and inhale her sweet scent or explore her lithe, luscious body.

Hell no. He wanted a double order of that all night long.

But time and circumstance slammed the door on any of that being a possibility. So all he could do was enjoy the moment and the chaste touches, then go home and take a freezing-cold shower.

Again.

"Jackson tells me you made the delicious wedding cake," he said, keeping things polite even as his imagination was peeling her pretty blue dress down over those sexy shoulders.

"Thank you." She blushed prettily as her hand settled on his shoulder, and warmth nestled in his chest. "Charli originally ordered one from a bakery in Austin. But along with all the other disasters she had to deal with, the bakery burned down."

"So I heard." While others on the dance floor twirled in wide sweeps to the music, he and Fiona danced in place—thighs brushing together with perfect synchronization. Hearts beating in time. He couldn't help but wonder if they'd have that same harmony between the sheets. "Guess their determination to go through with the wedding after all the mishaps is a testament to how the rest of their marriage will go."

Her sexy chuckle rumbled against his chest.

"I'm not worried about that. Have you met Charli?" She looked up at him, and the impish curl of her lips sent a flutter through his stomach. "When there's something she wants, she is like an unstoppable force. And she *wanted* Reno."

"You have to admire a woman who won't let anything stand in her way." A lively couple bumped him from behind, and he took the opportunity to draw Fiona into his body a little closer. In a blink, he realized the move might have been a huge tactical error. And that was not an egotistical observation on the size of his dick. Although the body part in question was exactly the problem that had come up.

Aside from the sheer sexiness level, Fiona was the kind of woman a man wanted to adore and savor. To possess and protect. To make her his very own and never let her go. Crazy talk coming from a guy like him. But for whatever reason, he couldn't stop himself.

"I also heard you're planning to open a cupcake shop in Sweet," he said without missing a beat. "That's quite a bold venture."

"It's been a longtime dream for me. Seeing it become a reality is going to be amazing. Izzy and I are even moving to Sweet to make it happen."

"So what inspired the dream?" he asked, hoping the band would play an extended version of the song so he could keep her talking. And moving against him.

The spark of enthusiasm in her deep blue eyes propelled a thousand questions through his mind.

More than a mild curiosity existed where she was concerned. He wanted to know more about her. What made her tick? What did she love and hold dear to her heart? And how, if she'd seen fit to divorce Jackson, they could remain as bonded as peanut butter and jelly?

A sentimental smile lifted the corners of her mouth. "My grandmother."

As she spoke, Mike noted how animated her face became. It was like observing one of those Disney princesses he'd been forced to watch with his sisters over and over. Her eyes lit up, and she got this dreamy expression that sent his jaded heart into cartwheels.

Fiona Wilder fascinated him. And he doubted there'd ever been a man who wanted a woman more.

As the song ended, and she slipped from his arms, he suffered a sense of loss he'd be hard to compare.

"Thank you for the dance," she said with the slightest tilt of her head. Her silky blond hair slipped across one slender shoulder, and he couldn't help but reach out and smooth it back.

"My pleasure. I hope we'll have the chance to meet again," he said, refraining from a princely bow or a kiss on her hand that would only serve to make him look like an infatuated ass.

"Me too." She smiled again, something she did often and with incredible ease.

"In the meantime, if you ever need anything . . ." He winked. "Just dial 911."

About the Author

CANDIS TERRY was born and raised near the sunny beaches of Southern California and now makes her home on an Idaho farm. She's experienced life in such diverse ways as working in a Hollywood recording studio to chasing down wayward steers. Only one thing has remained the same: her passion for writing stories about relationships, the push and pull in the search for love, and the security one finds in their own happily-ever-after.

Discover great authors, exclusive offers, and more at hc.com.

Give in to your impulses . . .
Read on for a sneak peek at five brand-new
e-book original tales of romance
from Avon Impulse.
Available now wherever e-books are sold.

An Excerpt from

VARIOUS STATES OF UNDRESS: VIRGINIA

by Laura Simcox

If she had it her way, Virginia Fulton—daughter of
the President of the United States—would spend
more time dancing in Manhattan's nightclubs than
working in its skyscrapers. But when she finds
herself in the arms of sexy, persuasive Dexter
Cameron, who presents her with the opportunity
of a lifetime, Virginia sees it as a sign . . . but
can she take it without losing her heart?

Virginia threw her hands in the air and walked over to face him. "Come on, Dex! Be realistic. You need a *team* to fix this store. An army."

"So hire one." He leaned toward her. "I need you. And you need me."

"I don't need you." She narrowed her eyes. There was no way she was going to tell him about dumping Owlton. Not right now, anyway.

Dex slid off the desk and covered the few feet between them, frowning. "Yes, you do," he said.

She stared at his mouth, her legs suddenly feeling wobbly. "No, I don't." She raised her hands to his shoulders to steady herself.

"You can choose to keep telling yourself that, or you can make a move."

"What do you mean by that?"

"Move forward."

She took a deep breath. "I don't know if I can." The words came out raspy, and the look of irritation in Dex's eyes changed into something much more focused. He hesitated for a moment and then leaned closer. "Make a leap of faith, trust your instincts, and take the job. You'll have my full support."

As she gazed up into his steady eyes, she was all too aware of her fear. Because of cowardice, she never acted as if she expected anyone to take her seriously—and so they didn't. It pissed her off. She didn't like being pissed, especially not at herself. Dex took her seriously, didn't he? She closed her eyes. "Okay. I'll do it."

When she opened them, he smiled. "Great. Now . . . about moving forward?"

"Yeah?"

"*Literally* moving forward would be fantastic. I never got to kiss you back, you know."

"I . . . didn't expect you to," she said.

"That might be, but the more I thought about your kiss last night, the more necessary kissing you back became to me. And now? I can't think about much else."

She gripped his shoulders and gazed into his eyes. "To be honest, neither can I."

"Please tell me we can try again. Kiss me and see what happens." His voice was low and thick.

Virginia's legs almost gave out from under her, and a shuddering breath left her body. She should be taking a step back, not contemplating kissing him again. Her body swayed forward, and she tightened her grip on his shoulders to steady herself. Just as she closed her eyes to think, his mouth descended, hot and sweet, angling over hers and stopping a hairsbreadth from her lips.

"Mmm," he uttered, the sound coming from deep in his throat, and it was all she needed.

She pushed up onto her toes, her fingers laced behind his neck, and she kissed him. He tasted earthy—wild, almost—

and that surprising discovery sent a shock wave through her brain. She kissed him again. "More," she murmured, even though she knew she shouldn't. His tongue invaded her mouth; he turned and, in one motion, lifted her onto the desk. Electricity sang through her body, and, as she twined her tongue with his, the idea of *shouldn't* started to become hazy. Her hands threaded through his cropped hair and she leaned back—arching her breasts toward him—wanting Dex to press her down with his body. *Please*, she whispered in her mind, *Please, Dex*.

His hands ran over her hips, but he didn't move closer, so she deepened the kiss, letting her hands trail over his smooth jaw, the taut sides of his neck; then she slid her fingers around the lapels of his suit and tugged. With a groan, Dex pulled her against his chest again, his hands skimming up her back to gently tug on the blunt ends of her hair. She complied, letting her head fall back, and his hot, open mouth slid down her throat and nestled in the crook of her neck. He kissed her there, lingering.

"More," she gasped out loud, clinging to his shoulders.

He kissed her throat again, his tongue branding a circle under her jaw. Then slowly, he pulled away. "We have to stop," he said, looking into her eyes. "If we don't . . ." He swallowed and she watched his throat work. She hadn't gotten to kiss him there, yet. Dipping her chin, she leaned forward, but he pulled away. He gave her a sheepish smile. "I think we sealed the deal, don't you?

An Excerpt from

THE GOVERNESS CLUB: LOUISA

by Ellie Macdonald

Louisa Brockhurst is on the run—from her friends, from her family, even from her dream of independence through the Governess Club. Handsome but menacing John Taylor is a prizefighter-turned-innkeeper who is trying to make his way in society. When Louisa shows up at his doorstep, he's quick to accept her offer to help—at a price. Their attraction grows, but will headstrong, fiery Louisa ever trust the surprisingly kind John enough to tell him the dangerous secrets from her past that keep her running?

Her eyes followed his movements as he straightened. Good Lord, but the moniker "Giant Johnny" was highly appropriate. The man was a mountain. A fleeting thought crossed her mind about what it would be like to have those large arms encompass her.

He spied her packed portmanteau and looked at her questioningly. "You are moving on? I thought your plans were unconfirmed."

Louisa lifted her chin. "They are. But that does not mean I must stay here in order to solidify them."

He put his thick hands on his hips, doubling his width. "But it also means that you do not have to leave in order to do so." She opened her mouth to speak, but he stayed her with his hand. "I understand what it is like to be adrift. If you wish, you can remain here. It is clear that I need help, a woman's help." He gestured to the room. "I have little notion and less inclination for cleaning. I need someone to take charge in this area. Will you do it?"

Louisa stared at him. *Help him by being a maid? In an inn?* Of all the things she had considered doing, working in such a place had never crossed her mind. She was not suited for such work. A governess, a companion, yes—but a maid?

What would her mother have said about this? Or any of her family?

She pressed her lips together. It had been six years since she'd allowed her family to influence her, and this job would at least keep her protected from the elements. She would be able to protect herself from the more unruly patrons, she was certain. It would be hard-earned coin, to be sure, but the current condition of her moneybag would not object to whichever manner she earned more. It would indeed present the biggest challenge she had yet faced, but how hard could it be?

"What say you, Mrs. Brock?"

His voice drew her out of her thoughts. Regarding him carefully, Louisa knew better than just to accept his offer. "What sorts of benefits could I expect?"

"Proper wage, meals, and a room." His answer was quick.

"How many meals?"

"How many does the average person eat?" he countered. "Three by my count."

Would her stomach survive three meals of such fare? She nodded. "This room? Or a smaller one in the attic?" She had slept in her fair share of small rooms as a governess; she would fight for the biggest one she could get.

"This one is fine. This is not a busy inn, so it can be spared." He rubbed his bald head. "My room is behind the office, so you will never be alone on the premises."

Hm. "I see. Free days?" Not that she expected to need them. She knew no one in the area and had no plans to inform her friends—her *former* friends—of where she was.

"Once a fortnight."

"And my duties?"

"Cleaning, of course. Helping out in the kitchen and pub when necessary."

"Was last night a typical crowd?" she asked.

"Yes. Local men come here regularly. There are not many places a man in this area can go."

"And the women? I am curious."

He shrugged his boulder shoulders. "None have yet come in here. I don't cater to their tastes."

Louisa sniffed and glanced around the room. The condition truly was atrocious. If the other rooms were like this, it would take days of hard work to get them up to scratch. It would be an accomplishment to be proud of, if she succeeded.

Ha—if I succeed? I always succeed.

She looked back at Giant Johnny, watching her with his hands on his hips, legs braced apart. She eyed him. He stood like a sportsman, sure of his ground and his strength. A sliver of awareness slipped through her at the confidence he exuded. This man was capable of many things; she was certain of it.

And if she were to agree to his offer, she would be with him every day. This mountain, this behemoth, would have authority over her as her employer. It was not the proximity to the giant that worried her; it was that last fact.

It rankled. For so long she had wished for independence, had almost achieved it with her friends and the formation of the Governess Club, only to have it collapse underneath her. And now she found herself once again having to submit to a man's authority.

It was a bitter pill to swallow. She would have to trust that she would eventually be able to turn the situation to her advantage. Nodding, she said, "I accept the position, Mr. Taylor."

An Excerpt from

GOOD GUYS WEAR BLACK

by Lizbeth Selvig

When single mom Rose Hanrahan arrives in
Kennison Falls, Minnesota, as the new head
librarian, she instantly clashes with hometown
hero Dewey Mitchell over just about everything.
But in a small town like Kennison Falls,
it's tough to ignore anybody, and the more
they're thrown together, the more it seems
like fate has something in store for them.

Waves of anger, like blasts of heat, rolled off the woman as she turned to the pumps. Rooted to the spot, Dewey watched the scene, studying the mystifying child. He was standing a little too close to the gas fumes, but irritation took a reluctant backseat to curiosity and captivation. What kind of kid couldn't follow a simple directive from people in uniform? What nine- or ten-year-old kid knew the year, make, and model of a fourteen-year-old fire truck, not to mention its specs—right down to the capacities of its foam firefighting equipment?

Asperger's syndrome. He knew the phrase but little about it. He certainly believed there were real syndromes out there, since he'd seen plenty of strange behavior in his life. But this reeked of a pissed-off mother simply warning him away from her weird kid. He knew in this day and age you weren't supposed to touch a child, but, damn it, the kid could have gotten seriously hurt. And she sure as hell hadn't been around.

Then there was the car. Over ten years old and spotless as new. The red GT did *not* fit the woman. Or the situation. You just didn't expect to see a mom and her son driving cross-country in a fireball-red sports car. She had some sort of mild, uppity accent and used words like "ire." In a way, she wasn't any more normal than her kid.

He tried to turn away. She wasn't from town, so he wouldn't have to think about her once the gas was pumped. But something compelled him to watch her finish—something that told him the world would go back to being a lot less interesting once she'd left it.

She let the boy hang the nozzle up, and then did something amazing. She opened her door, took out what appeared to be a chamois, and bent over the gas tank door to wipe and buff an area where gas must have dripped.

She doesn't deserve it if she doesn't know how to take care of it. That's what he'd said about her.

Dang. She sure knew how to keep it . . . red.

His observations were cut off by a sudden wail. The boy lunged like a spaniel after a squirrel. The woman grabbed him, squatted, and took his hands in hers, pressing his palms together like he was praying. Her mouth moved quickly, and she leaned in close, her forehead nearly but not quite touching her son's.

It should not have been a remotely sexy picture, but it was nearly as attractive as the sight of her polishing the Mustang. The over-reactive Mama Wolverine morphed into someone intense and sincere with desperation around the edges, and something he didn't understand at all tugged at him, deep in his gut.

The boy finally nodded and quit fussing. The woman dropped her hands and leaned forward to kiss him on the cheek. After straightening, she glanced over her shoulder, and the boy's wistful gaze followed. Dewey remembered that he'd begged only to look at the gauges on the truck. Should he just give in and let the kid have his look?

Then everything soft about the mother hardened as she met Dewey's eyes. Her delicately angled features tightened like sharp weapons, and the wisps of hair escaping from a long, thick brown ponytail seemed to freeze in place as if they didn't dare move for fear of pissing her off further. She stood, her shapely legs—their calves bare and browned beneath the hems of knee-length cargo shorts—spread like a superhero's in front of her son. She didn't say a word, so neither did Dewey. He didn't need to take her on again. Let the kid look up the gauges online.

With a parting shot from her angry eyes, she ushered the boy into the passenger seat, darted to her side, and climbed in. The engine came to life and purred like a jungle cat. She clearly cared for the car the way she did for her son. Or somebody did.

However angry she was, she didn't take it out on the car but pulled smoothly away from the pump. Dewey smiled. It was her car all right. Had it not been, she'd have peeled out just to punctuate her feelings for him.

Impressive woman. A little crazy. But impressive.

An Excerpt from

SINFUL REWARDS 1
A Billionaires and Bikers Novella
by Cynthia Sax

Belinda "Bee" Carter is a good girl; at least, that's
what she tells herself. And a good girl deserves
a nice guy—just like the gorgeous and moody
billionaire Nicolas Rainer. Or so she thinks,
until she takes a look through her telescope
and sees a naked, tattooed man on the balcony
across the courtyard. He has been watching
her, and that makes him all the more enticing.
But when a mysterious and anonymous text
message dares her to do something bad, she
must decide if she is really the good girl she has
always claimed to be, or if she's willing to risk
everything for her secret fantasy of being watched.

An Avon Red Novella

I'd told Cyndi I'd never use it, that it was an instrument purchased by perverts to spy on their neighbors. She'd laughed and called me a prude, not knowing that I was one of those perverts, that I secretly yearned to watch and be watched, to care and be cared for.

If I'm cautious, and I'm always cautious, she'll never realize I used her telescope this morning. I swing the tube toward the bench and adjust the knob, bringing the mysterious object into focus.

It's a phone. Nicolas's phone. I bounce on the balls of my feet. This is a sign, another declaration from fate that we belong together. I'll return Nicolas's much-needed device to him. As a thank you, he'll invite me to dinner. We'll talk. He'll realize how perfect I am for him, fall in love with me, marry me.

Cyndi will find a fiancé also—everyone loves her—and we'll have a double wedding, as sisters of the heart often do. It'll be the first wedding my family has had in generations.

Everyone will watch us as we walk down the aisle. I'll wear a strapless white Vera Wang mermaid gown with organza and lace details, crystal and pearl embroidery accents, the bodice fitted, and the skirt hemmed for my shorter height. My hair will be swept up. My shoes—

Voices murmur outside the condo's door, the sound piercing my delightful daydream. I swing the telescope upward, not wanting to be caught using it. The snippets of conversation drift away.

I don't relax. If the telescope isn't positioned in the same way as it was last night, Cyndi will realize I've been using it. She'll tease me about being a fellow pervert, sharing the story, embellished for dramatic effect, with her stern, serious dad—or, worse, with Angel, that snobby friend of hers.

I'll die. It'll be worse than being the butt of jokes in high school because that ridicule was about my clothes and this will center on the part of my soul I've always kept hidden. It'll also be the truth, and I won't be able to deny it. I am a pervert.

I have to return the telescope to its original position. This is the only acceptable solution. I tap the metal tube.

Last night, my man-crazy roommate was giggling over the new guy in three-eleven north. The previous occupant was a gray-haired, bowtie-wearing tax auditor, his luxurious accommodations supplied by Nicolas. The most exciting thing he ever did was drink his tea on the balcony.

According to Cyndi, the new occupant is a delicious piece of man candy—tattooed, buff, and head-to-toe lickable. He was completing armcurls outside, and she enthusiastically counted his reps, oohing and aahing over his bulging biceps, calling to me to take a look.

I resisted that temptation, focusing on making macaroni and cheese for the two of us, the recipe snagged from the diner my mom works in. After we scarfed down dinner, Cyndi licking her plate clean, she left for the club and hasn't returned.

Three-eleven north is the mirror condo to ours. I

straighten the telescope. That position looks about right, but then, the imitation UGGs I bought in my second year of college looked about right also. The first time I wore the boots in the rain, the sheepskin fell apart, leaving me barefoot in Economics 201.

Unwilling to risk Cyndi's friendship on "about right," I gaze through the eyepiece. The view consists of rippling golden planes, almost like . . .

Tanned skin pulled over defined abs.

I blink. It can't be. I take another look. A perfect pearl of perspiration clings to a puckered scar. The drop elongates more and more, stretching, snapping. It trickles downward, navigating the swells and valleys of a man's honed torso.

No. I straighten. This is wrong. I shouldn't watch our sexy neighbor as he stands on his balcony. If anyone catches me . . .

Parts 1, 2, 3, and 4 available now!

An Excerpt from

COVERING KENDALL
A Love and Football Novel
by Julie Brannagh

Kendall Tracy, General Manager of the San
Francisco Miners, is not one for rash decisions
or one-night stands. But when she finds herself
alone in a hotel room with a heart-stoppingly
gorgeous man—who looks oddly familiar—
Kendall throws her own rules out the window . . .

Drew McCoy *should* look familiar; he's a star player
for her team's archrival, the Seattle Sharks.
They agree to pretend their encounter never
happened. But staying away from each
other is harder than it seems, and they both
discover that some risks are worth taking.

An Excerpt from

COVERING KENDALL

A Love and Football Novel

by Julie Brannagh

"You're Drew McCoy," she cried out.

She scooted to the edge of the bed, clutching the sheet around her torso as she went. It was a little late now for modesty. Retaining some shred of dignity might be a good thing.

She'd watched Drew's game film with the coaching staff. She'd seen his commercials for hair products and sports drinks and soup a hundred times before. His contract with the Sharks was done as of the end of football season, and the Miners wanted him to play for them. Drew was San Francisco's number-one target in next season's free agency. She'd planned on asking the team's owner to write a big check to Drew and his agent next March. And if all that wasn't enough, Drew was eight years younger than she was.

What the hell was wrong with her? It must have been the knit hat covering his famous hair, or finding him in a non-jock hangout like a bookstore. Maybe it was the temporary insanity brought on by an overwhelming surge of hormones.

"Is there a problem?" he said.

"I can't have anything to do with you. I have to go."

He shook his head in adorable confusion. She couldn't think of anything she wanted more right now than to run her fingers through his gorgeous hair.

"This is your hotel room. Where do you think you're going?"

She yanked as much of the sheet off the bed as possible, attempting to wrap it around herself and stand up at the same time. He was simultaneously grabbing at the comforter to shield himself. It didn't work.

She twisted her foot in the bedding while she hurled herself away from him and ended up on the carpet seconds later in a tangle of sheets and limbs, still naked. Her butt hit the floor so hard she almost expected to bounce.

The number-one reason Kendall didn't engage in one-night stands as a habit hauled himself up on all fours in the middle of the bed. Out of all the guys in the world available for a short-term fling, of *course* she'd pick the man who could get her fired or sued.

He grabbed the robe he'd slung over the foot of the bed, scrambled off the mattress, and jammed his arms into the sleeves as he advanced on her.

"Are you okay? You went down pretty hard." His eyes skimmed over her. "That's going to leave a mark."

He crouched next to her as he reached out to help her up. She resisted the impulse to stare at golden skin, an eight-pack, and a sizable erection. She'd heard Drew didn't lack for dates. He had things to offer besides the balance in his bank accounts.

"I'm okay," she told him.

She felt a little shaky. She'd probably have a nice bruise later. She was going down all right, and it had nothing to do with sex. It had everything to do with the fact that, if anyone from the Miners organization saw him emerging from her room in the next seventy-two hours, she was in the kind of trouble with her employer there was no recovering from. The interim general manager of an NFL team did not sleep with anyone from the opposing team, especially when the two teams were archrivals that hated each other with the heat of a thousand suns. Especially when the guy was a star player her own organization was more than a little interested in acquiring. *Especially* before a game that could mean the inside track to the playoffs for both teams.

Drew and Kendall would be the Romeo and Juliet of the NFL. Well, without all the dying. Death by 24/7 sports media embarrassment didn't count.

He reached out, grabbed her beneath the armpits, and hoisted her off the floor like she weighed nothing.

"I've got you. Let's see if you can stand up," he said. His warm, gentle hands moved over her, looking for injuries. "Why don't you lean on me for a second here?"

She tried rewrapping the sheet around her so she could walk away from him while preserving her dignity. It wasn't going to happen. She couldn't stop staring at him. If she let him take her in his arms, she'd be lost. She teetered as she leaned against the hotel room wall.

"I'm—I'm fine. I—"

"Hold still," he said. She heard his bare feet slap against the carpeting as he grabbed the second robe out of the coat closet and brought it back to her. "If you don't want to do this, that's your decision, but I don't understand what's wrong."

She struggled into the thick terry robe as she tried to think of a response. He was staring at her as she retrieved the belt and swathed herself in yards of fabric. Judging by his continuing erection, he liked what he saw, even if it was covered up from her neck to below her knees. He licked his bottom lip. Her mouth went dry. Damn it.

Of *course* the most attractive guy she'd been anywhere near a bed with in the past year was completely off-limits.

"You don't recognize me," she said.

"No, I don't," he said. "Is there a problem?"

"You might say that." She finally succeeded in knotting the belt of the robe around her waist, dropped the sheet at her feet, and stuck out one hand. "Hi. I'm Kendall Tracy. I'm the interim GM of the San Francisco Miners." His eyes widened in shock. "Nice to meet you."